Living in Imperial Rome

by Eilís Dillon

**WINNER OF
Irish Children's Book Trust
BISTO AWARD 1991**

'An excellent book for children, describing life in that
great capital city, in very human and living terms,
as if it were yesterday'
BAPTIST TIMES

Eilís Dillon was born in Galway in 1920. She is an
internationally renowned and award-winning author
for children and adults. Her books have been
translated into many language.

Living in Imperial Rome

EILÍS DILLON

Illustrated by Richard Kennedy

THE O'BRIEN PRESS
DUBLIN

First paperback edition published 1991
by The O'Brien Press Ltd.,
20 Victoria Road, Dublin 6, Ireland.

First published in hardback 1972
by Faber and Faber London.

10 9 8 7 6 5 4 3 2 1

British Library Cataloguing in Publication Data
Dillon, Eilis, 1920 -
Living in imperial Rome.
I. Title II. Kennedy, Richard, 1910
823-914
ISBN 0-86278-264-3

The O'Brien Press receives assistance from
the Arts Council/An Chomhairle Ealaíon.

Cover illustration: Donald Teskey
Cover Separations: The City Office, Dublin
Printing: The Guernsey Press Co. Ltd.

Contents

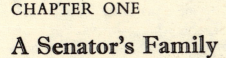

CHAPTER ONE

A Senator's Family

It is a warm June morning in the year A.D. 110, the thirteenth year of the reign of the Emperor Trajan. This is the best time of the day. Even the smells that pervade the City seem a little less obnoxious than they will do later, when the heat will become almost unbearable.

The City is at peace just now. The recent wars have all been successful and everyone has a comfortable feeling of getting a share of the loot. More wars are planned, so continued prosperity can be expected. The Emperor is an active, successful ruler. He can be trusted to spread the glory of Rome to the ends of the earth. Distant wars are always preferable to those that come near home, and fortunately the conquered countries whose wealth pours into Italy are a month's journey away.

In his fine house on the Aventine Hill, the Senator Flavius and his family are getting up. Flavius is very rich and important, and owns hundreds of slaves. Those among them who work in the house have been up and about since the dawn, cleaning the rooms and the courtyard. They work fast and well, to have everything in order by the time their master appears. He likes to take a stroll about the house and look over everything himself before he begins to dress. As he has a habit of keeping his whip at the ready, it is well to be safely finished and out of the way before he arrives.

Yet Flavius is not a bad master, on the whole. He feeds his slaves properly and their sleeping quarters are dry and warm in winter. Besides, as well as noticing when work is badly done, he notices when someone does things well, and he is generous with rewards of money. When he frees his slaves, they always have a nest-egg to start them in business, or, if they continue to work for him, to buy slaves of their own.

While they work, the slaves make a great noise of banging and shouting, pulling ladders about as they clean down the walls, shifting furniture and beating mats and opening shutters with a clatter. Almost before they have finished, the first of the clients have begun to arrive.

These clients are hangers-on of the Senator, and they come every morning to pay their respects to him while he dresses. Each one brings half a dozen slaves with him, either to carry his litter or just to walk beside him. Carriages are not allowed inside the walls of the City. Most of the visitors have clients of their own, and have already held court for them at their own houses, an hour ago.

The Senator must greet his clients and ask about their families and promise to pull strings for them if he can, later in the day. A poor client has to be given some money or even a new toga. Each one must be invited to dinner now and then and he must get a fat present from Flavius in December, as well.

While he talks, the clients ramble in and out of his bedroom. He sleeps alone. His wife has a room in another part of the house.

Meanwhile Flavius' son Lucius has been getting up and dressing in his own room. The racket made by the slaves woke him up, and he called for his own slave, who is also his tutor, to tell him that he is ready to dress.

First the heavy wooden shutters are opened and as there is no glass in the window, the fresh, clean air fills the room. Birds are singing in the garden and the fountain is playing in the sunshine. In June it is very pleasant to wake up but even in winter Lucius would not think of lying in bed.

His dressing is very simple. He has slept in most of the clothes he wears—a loin-cloth and a loose, short-sleeved tunic made of linen with a belt at the waist. In winter this tunic would be made of wool. He arranges it by means of the belt so that the front is a little shorter than the back.

The slave fetches his sandals, which consist of a leather sole, tied around the ankles with leather thongs. Then comes the more difficult task of putting on the toga. Lucius was fifteen years old in March, so he is now entitled to wear a man's toga, and he fidgets nervously while his slave gets it right.

Lucius has always worn a toga, but until he was fifteen it was a lighter one, white with a purple border. The toga he wears now is a much more difficult problem. It is a big circle of white woollen cloth, awkward to wear and hard to keep clean but well worth the trouble for the style it gives its wearer. It has to be folded in a certain way, with a collection of pleats on one shoulder which so far Lucius can only keep in place by having that shoulder slightly hunched. It reaches to his heels, and altogether he finds it an uncomfortable and irritating garment. Still, though he need not really wear it until he goes out he thinks it worth while to get accustomed to it. Otherwise he would despair of ever wearing it with the careless, dramatic air of the older men.

Lucius does not bother to wash much. The slave brings him a silver bowl of water with which he splashes his face and hands. Later in the day, when he goes to the baths, he will wash so thoroughly that he feels no need to wash now.

He takes no breakfast except a glass of water. His first meal will be at noon, since his father is rather old-fashioned and believes in keeping the habits of the founders of Rome, in some things at least. He often talks of the decadence of modern society and says that Romans should remember that their city was founded by the plough; but Lucius notices that his father soon gets bored when they go to the country in summer and is always looking for an excuse to come in to the city.

When he is ready, Lucius leaves his bedroom and goes out to mix with the crowd of clients in the hall. His slave, who is dressed exactly as Lucius is, except for the toga, goes with him. On his way, Lucius calls at the latrine which is placed off the entrance-hall. This is a great and convenient luxury, only to be found in the house of a very rich man.

As soon as they have gone, two house slaves come in and clean the bedroom and make the bed. This consists of strips of interwoven webbing on a carved wooden base, with a wool mattress and pillow. There are two blankets, and Lucius gets between them when he goes to bed. If he feels cold, he can put his toga on top. He has a fine embroidered quilt which came from Arabia last year, and his bedside rug is Persian, soft and intricately patterned. The slaves shake the bedclothes and the rug out of the window before putting them back in their places.

In an inner room of the house, Lucius' sister Cornelia is getting up too. She is thirteen years old, and she does not have to dress elaborately, but she makes her slave hurry with tying her sandals so that she will be in time to watch her mother dress. Cornelia enjoys this spectacle very much, and though she knows the routine very well, still she always watches carefully as she will have to be able to do the same herself quite soon.

Cornelia's slave is not very efficient. She is Arabian and she finds it difficult to understand Latin. When she came to the house a year ago, she was put to work in the laundry and no one bothered to teach her anything. Or perhaps she was too frightened to learn. She was one of the fifty thousand prisoners that the Emperor brought back from the wars and she was only seventeen then. She had seen her father and her brothers killed, and though she knows that her mother was brought to Rome too, she has not heard any news of her yet.

Cornelia has given her a lovely Roman name, Livia, and has begun to teach her Latin so that they can talk and enjoy themselves together. Cornelia told her that her old name was barbaric, but fortunately Livia did not understand what she said. Livia's father was an important man in his own country, and until the Romans came and took her away, she had servants of her own. She is fond of Cornelia, who is obviously very friendly, and never hits her nor knocks her down while her shoes are being tied.

Livia finds life in the Senator's house interesting and she is trying to forget to hate the Romans all the time for what they did to her family. Besides, she knows she has been lucky. In the slaves' quarters she hears fearful stories of the treatment that some have had. She has decided that the best thing to do is to settle down to her new life and be as Roman as possible.

Like her brother, Cornelia has worn her loin-cloth and tunic in bed. Under the tunic she wears also a brassière and a corset. Over all this she now slips a long outer tunic that reaches to her heels and is belted at the waist. For going out, she has a palla, which is a rectangular piece of woollen cloth with a hole for her head, but she does not bother with it now. She gives her face a sketchy wash while Livia holds the bowl of water. Then, when her hair is done, they go to her mother's room.

When they arrive, the room seems full of people because of the confusion and running to and fro. As soon as they are inside, the door is locked in case Flavius might take it into his head to pay a call on his wife in her room. It would never do if he were to see her before her make-up is completed.

Flavius' wife Julia is like her husband, rather kind-hearted.

11

Sometimes she lets her temper go but on the whole she is concerned to give a good example to Cornelia so that she will grow up with the exterior virtues of a Roman matron—calm and steady and unruffled even in the face of the greatest misfortune.

Livia makes sure to be as quiet as a mouse in Julia's room. In the slaves' quarters, she has heard stories of enraged ladies flying at their dressing-women with whips or stunning them with a blow of a heavy mirror. Again she thinks how lucky she is to have been bought by a civilised household.

She can't help noticing, however, that Julia's dressing-woman looks very nervous. She does everything precisely but with no appearance of hurry. When the two girls arrive, she is arranging Julia's hair. This is an extra-elaborate business, as Julia is going to the Forum this morning to make her will, and for this she feels she should be finely dressed.

Watching the process, Cornelia thinks how much better it would be if she could always wear her own hair as comfortably as she does now, parted in the middle and pulled into a soft bun at the back of her neck. Her mother's hair has to be curled all over with tongs which are heated on a little charcoal stove. Then it is piled into a big soft mass on top of her head, with every curl neatly tucked in. The whole erection is lightly touched with oily hands to keep it in place, for Julia would be disgraced if it were to fall down in public. There is no real danger of this, since she has good, strong, dark hair. If she had not, she would undoubtedly wear a wig of black Indian hair, the most expensive kind.

It takes more than an hour to finish Julia's hair. Then begins the task of putting on her make-up, and this is what the girls like best to watch. There is no attempt to look natural. In fact it almost seems as if Julia wants to look rather like a marble statue, with colouring added here and there.

After she has splashed her face, it is dried carefully and then powdered over with a mixture of chalk and white lead. If she

12

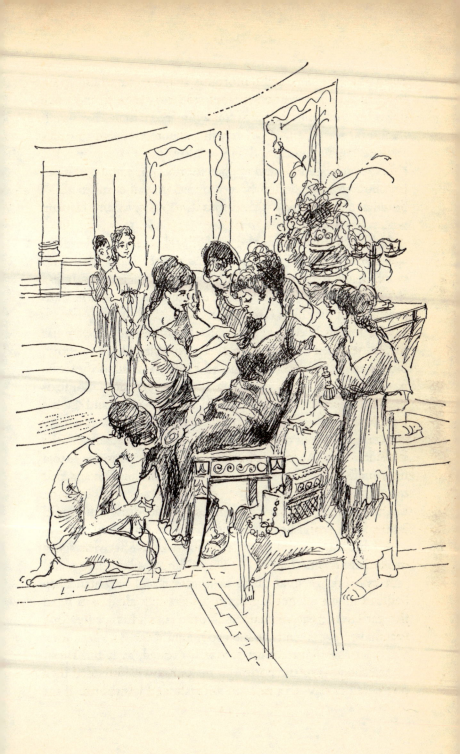

were going to spend the morning at home supervising her household or getting on with her spinning, Julia would leave out this part of the routine as the white lead irritates her skin if she uses it too often. However, she is quite prepared to suffer in order to make a good show. Now her maid paints her cheeks a delicate red, and applies some of the same colour to her lips. Another slightly poisonous metallic substance—powdered antimony—is used to outline her eyes and blacken her eyebrows.

Half an hour goes on this, and it will all have to be done again after Julia has been to the baths later in the day. Her maids have their hands full, between looking after Julia's clothes and taking care of all the equipment that goes into producing a dignified Roman lady.

Julia loves silk dresses, especially for going out in. She has fifteen or twenty of them, in every possible colour—yellow, blue, purple, red, pink, green and black. As well as these she has some fine Indian cotton ones, for lesser occasions. Some of the silk dresses are heavily embroidered with gold, and she has jewellery to match all these colours. The design of her dresses is always the same; only the material varies. Because she is the wife of a wealthy man of high rank, her dress is the "stola matronalis". This is a long tunic, reaching to her feet and tied by a belt at the waist.

Today Julia is wearing a peacock-blue dress with gold embroidery around the hem, so she picks rings and earrings and a bracelet of gold, intricately worked. She has a gold ornament in her hair too. The Chinese silk glitters and reflects specks of gold on its shining surface. Julia stands up and her maids put on her heavy yellow silk cloak and hand her her fan of peacock feathers. Cornelia and Livia agree that they have never seen Julia look so magnificent.

In fact she looks almost too well-dressed, as it turns out. When she goes to the Forum to make her will, attended by a dozen of her slaves, one of the witnesses is a lawyer noted for his meanness. He is so much impressed at the sight of Julia that he asks her to leave him her fine clothes in her will. Half-jokingly she agrees, but as the slaves carry her home in her litter, she remembers uneasily how the lawyer took the paper from her hand to read it himself and make sure she had really done as he asked. It's all very well to leave people things in your will, but there is no need for the beneficiaries to look so eager.

Long before Julia leaves the house, Flavius is on his way to the Forum. Before he goes, he spends a few minutes at the shrine where images of the household gods are ranged around an altar. They are Vesta, the goddess of fire, the Penates who guard the house, and the Lares who guard the family's land. He prays to them for success in today's affairs. If something extra important were planned, or if it were a special festival, the whole family would assemble to offer sacrifice. Lucius always attends very carefully to religious rites, so that he will be able to carry them out himself when he is older. Almost since they could walk, he and his sister have been acting as acolytes. A few months ago, when he received the man's toga, sacrifice was offered at the shrine to the household gods and his boy's toga was dedicated to them in a special ceremony.

This morning, when the clients have left, Lucius goes with his tutor to the Forum. His tutor is a Greek. Lucius does not think much of the Greeks but unfortunately they are the best teachers, and he must put up with them if he is to get any education. At home Lucius speaks Latin, but all higher education is done through Greek. When he was younger his tutor taught him at home. He knows from talking to other boys that this was a lot pleasanter than going to an elementary school.

Since the day when Lucius put on his man's toga, he is almost completely his own master. He hopes to be a barrister and eventually a Senator, like his father. As there are nine hundred Senators in Rome he is quite likely to succeed. For this he must above all learn rhetoric, which is really the art of making a long and complicated speech on any subject under the sun. His father has found him an excellent teacher, also a Greek, who holds classes every day for boys of Lucius' age.

This teacher will not teach him to think, however, unless he is lucky. Philosophy has been frowned on in Rome for the last two or three hundred years. It is considered unpatriotic to speculate on whether new ideas might be better than old. The Christians know this to their cost. Their greatest crime is in their suggestion that Rome and the Roman gods are not the most powerful. Rome and its ways have dominated the universe, which surely proves that they are the best of all. The Consul Pompey had his last Triumph in 61 B.C., over the third division of the world. The first was over Africa, the second over Europe and the last over Asia.

Old men whose great-grandfathers saw this Triumph still talk of what they heard about the procession, which took two days to pass through the City. The names of the fifteen countries that Pompey had subdued were carried on placards for all to see. His prisoners of war, who were led in the procession, were kings and the wives and children of kings. The gold and silver he had captured made Rome rich. Pompey was a man of big ideas. In his first Triumph he had meant to have his chariot drawn by four elephants but the City gates were too narrow to admit them, so he had had to make do with horses. This is the ideal Roman, and Lucius feels that he cannot do better than follow in his footsteps.

Lucius has already done a good course in Greek literature with his tutor: lyric poetry, and the works of Homer and Aesop and the great playwrights. He has also had lessons in elocution, and the special, rather dramatic way of reciting pieces that he has learned by heart, which is useful now that he goes to the teacher of rhetoric.

All of Lucius' education is directed towards his making a

16

fine show, a good impression when he gets up to deliver a speech. The teacher never bothers about whether the piece they are studying contains any wisdom which might be turned to good account. His whole concern is to comment on the literary style, the use of metaphor and other figures of speech, and the building up of an effective climax.

As soon as he thinks his pupils have understood how to construct a piece of rhetoric, the teacher sets them to write essays which they will later have to declaim in public. The essay must be divided into six parts, and each of these parts must be developed according to a set pattern. The student is taught how to use syllogisms, that is to argue from two given propositions, called the premises, to a conclusion. An example would be: "All fathers are men; this is my father; therefore he is a man." It doesn't always work, however. Another example could be: "All crows are black; this is a black bird; therefore this is a crow." For style in an argument, the student is encouraged to use sets of three examples, three adjectives, or perhaps three descriptions, to give the sentence balance, and he must show that he understands how to give extra weight to a phrase by altering its position in the sentence. It is like a game and, as with all games, some people are better at it than others. Since Lucius has been listening to flowery speeches all his life he is quite an expert. His memory is well-developed, a very important point, as he must be able to give his speeches without notes.

Two kinds of subject are set by the teacher. One could just possibly be useful to a budding barrister, as it consists in defending or accusing an imaginary prisoner, but the teacher always makes sure that the cases are quite unreal. The second is a purely imaginary piece of speculation, purporting to take place in the mind of some remote historical character. In one discussion, for instance, one of the three hundred Spartans weighs the reasons for and against defending the Pass of Thermopylae to the last man. This is no more than an exercise in using the tricks he has been taught, and Lucius finds it rather amusing. He does not care when the teacher changes the facts of history to make a better discussion. In any case Lucius would probably not notice, as he has not been taught history accurately, nor any other subject either. Anything that looks or sounds well, anything that is aesthetically satisfying is tolerated, so why not change history if it makes a better story? Some of the legal cases that the teacher invents would be quite impossible in real life, and he commends any of his pupils who enter into the spirit of the thing and work their way through these fantastic situations, using the rules they have been taught.

Often some of the older men drop in to listen to the class, especially if the teacher is well-known. They enjoy it as an entertainment, and as an exhibition of skill, and perhaps this is why Lucius knows quite well that what he learns at school is not half as important for making him a useful Roman citizen as what he learns at home. At school he is being taught to talk, to express himself, to make an impression, as the teacher does. But being a Roman boy and not a Greek, he believes that what he says will always be more important than how he says it. His father often tells him this, and points out that an upright life is the most important thing to be cultivated, and he quotes Marcus Porcius Cato's saying: "Get hold of your subject and the words will follow." Though he is quick to learn the tricks, Lucius is beginning to find it all rather a bore and is impatient to be finished with school altogether.

He is glad that his classes take him to the Forum, however, because it is the centre of Rome and therefore of the whole world. It is exciting to remember that this is the very place where the great City was founded. Here the Romans fought the Sabines, and later made friends with them, and perhaps got the idea that an empire is best built up on friendship. The Tarpeian rock towers over the Forum, at the edge of the

Capitoline Hill. Since the foundation of the City it has been the custom to hurl traitors from this rock, and very properly the greatest of the gods, Jupiter, has his temple on the hill above it.

On this June morning the Forum is full of people. It gets hotter every moment, and everyone makes sure to keep in the shade as they go from one building to another. The class is over early, since some of the boys are beginning to fall asleep. Lucius comes out of the school, still followed by his slave, and decides to look for his father.

The first place he goes to is the Basilica Aemilia. His father often goes there to meet Marcus, the businessman who manages his affairs. Flavius has invested money in several of Marcus' schemes, and he talked a few days ago of selling him his new crop of wool from the flock that he keeps in Tusculum.

The Basilica is a huge hall with two side aisles, and Lucius walks from one group to another, enjoying the cool air. On the hottest day, it's cool in here. His father is not there, however. As he comes out, he glances along the line of money-changers' shops that are built against the front of the building, but he recognises none of their customers.

Keeping to the shade, he strolls along the Argiletum, the street where all the booksellers and copyists have their shops, until he comes to the Comitium. This place fascinates Lucius and he comes here most days, just to get the feel of it. This is where Romulus founded the Senate and it is the central meeting-place of the Roman people. The modern Senate House is nearby, and sometimes the senators come out and address the people from the great new rostrum that was built by Julius Caesar. Lucius shivers with fright as he imagines himself some day climbing into the rostrum and looking down on that mass of upturned faces. How will he fare then? Will he remember all the devices he has learned for keeping people's attention—the sudden roar of passion, the calling on the gods to witness, the dropping of the voice to a near whisper, the reasoned, clear argument and the peroration that will sum it all up?

He leaves the Comitium and turns into the Sacred Way. It is easier to walk here, as the street is paved with great stone blocks. This is the route that the Triumphs take, straight to the Temple of Jupiter, where at the end the victorious General sacrifices a pig, a goat and a bull. At the same time his vanquished enemies are executed in the prison which is built into the hill below. This seems disgusting to us, but Lucius is used to the idea, as he is to the traitors being hurled down to their death from the Tarpeian rock. Good enough for them, Lucius thinks, and as he doesn't intend ever to betray his country it really hasn't very much to do with him.

In two years' time he hopes to go to war. If he does well, captures a town, perhaps, or leads his men to victory on the battlefield, it will help him to get started on his career as a lawyer. He doesn't expect to be killed in battle himself, as he will be well protected by his own soldiers. Besides, it would be unworthy of a Roman citizen to think of such things.

Lucius never passes the Basilica Julia without stopping to have a look at what is going on there. This is the main law court, but since the Romans are always going to law, there are several others in full swing as well.

The Court of the Centumviri sits in the Basilica Julia. In spite of its name, which means "a hundred men", the judges are now one hundred and eighty in number. When they all sit together, as they are doing today, the presiding judge sits in the centre of the dais with ninety of his colleagues at either side. Close to the dais, the people who are suing each other sit on benches with their lawyers and their witnesses and friends. The people of Rome love to hear a good orator, so the rest of the huge hall is crammed with eager listeners. If the defence is conducted by Pliny, it is likely to go on all day. Pliny believes in a fine long speech which leaves no stone unturned, and he usually quotes great and learned men in support of his case. He is a great admirer of Cicero, whose longest speech he says was his best. Lucius has heard his father argue with Pliny that conciseness is a virtue in a speech but Pliny holds the exactly opposite view. Nothing is more delightful than magnitude, he says, whether in men or animals or even in trees, so long as everything is in proportion. He maintains that the same is true in speeches, so if his opening section, the exordium, is long, you can forecast that all six sections of the speech will be pretty lengthy. The Court of the Centumviri is not allowed to adjourn, which means that sometimes a single case can take all day, from dawn to dusk.

When Lucius comes in, the defence is being argued by Fabius Justus, a boring old man whose voice is too low to be heard by any except those near him. Beside Lucius, a little fat woman says angrily:

"He's talking to himself. I came all the way to hear who is going to inherit Tullia's money and it's as big a mystery as ever."

She begins to elbow her way in through the crowd. Up near the dais, a group of people bursts into cheers of applause from time to time. These are hired by Fabius Justus, as everyone well knows. Some of the crowd imitate them ironically and the whole business is held up until silence falls again.

As he watches, Lucius thinks that good health and a strong, carrying voice are the first requirements of a lawyer. He hopes he will never cut as poor a figure as Fabius does. Oddly enough, Fabius seems quite unaware of his deficiencies. He gazes around blankly with his chin in the air, looking down his long nose with half-shut eyes, and holding his shoulders well back to give his toga a more dramatic appearance. It occurs to Lucius that a thick skin may be another thing that a successful lawyer needs, but he hopes to manage without one.

At this stage of his reflections, he feels the need to get out of the Court House as fast as possible. Fortunately, just outside he meets his friend Gaius, who is also a student of rhetoric and planning to be a lawyer.

Gaius is at a loose end and looking rather bored. He is watching a game of draughts between two seedy-looking middle-aged men who are squatting on the broad top step of the Basilica. The pieces are chips of black and white marble and the board is scratched on the step. These are professional applauders waiting to be hired by some lawyer, and Gaius, who is more practical and less idealistic than Lucius, is getting to know the good ones already. What he doesn't know is that they have spotted him too, and will be lying in wait for him, hoping for a job, the first time he makes his appearance in Court.

The two boys continue on their way, in the general direction of the Senate House. This is called the Curia, and was built by Julius Caesar. The Senate meets here twice every month, for ten months of the year. Lucius has been in the Curia with his father several times, but not of course during sessions. His father is very proud of his position as a Senator, shough the whole family keeps well out of his way whenever the sessions are on, because then he is liable to burst into flaming temper with little or no provocation. He hates to be cooped up day after day, from morning till night, and yet he would not miss a session for the world. Four or five hours for a speech is a common affair, and if Pliny is there it can be much more. Fortunately the Senators can go out for a breath of air during the sessions, much as Members of Parliament do nowadays.

Strolling around the Forum today, one can hardly imagine that such important things are happening so nearby. In the little booths of the tradesmen, goldsmiths and silversmiths are at work, making complicated rings and necklaces and other ornaments, the leather merchants are making sandals for men and women, the ivory sellers are carving figures of gods and animals, the flower-stalls have great masses of flowers on show, and the druggists are selling the perfumes that they make from recipes that have been handed down from generation to generation for hundreds of years.

Only luxury stalls are allowed in the Forum now. In ancient times, before real civilisation began, there were grocers and butchers and wine-merchants and various other unsavoury businesses carried on here. Now this would be considered beneath the dignity of the Forum, and only ornamental shops are allowed, where ladies may stroll and finger and admire and buy a new silly little thing almost every day, to vary the idle monotony of their lives. This morning Lucius' mother Julia has bought a finely worked cameo set in gold, to comfort her for the unpleasant thoughts connected with making her will. It is carved from a pink shell from Naples, and represents the goddess Diana with a team of hunting dogs.

Lucius and Gaius are beginning to get hungry, and they decide to go home to lunch, promising to meet at the baths later in the day. Lucius knows that a good Roman should be able to go all day without food if necessary. This was how the great Empire was built up, by men so tough that they never thought of their own comfort. All the same he finds that he is always hungry, and he walks home very briskly, wondering what there will be to eat.

His slave Demetrius is still walking along behind him. Now that Gaius has gone, Lucius waits for Demetrius to catch up with him. This slave of his fascinates Lucius. He can never quite make out what goes on in his head. He always seems to accept whatever is happening, whether it is pleasant or unpleasant, as one accepts fluctuations in the weather. He is

a first-class servant and valet. He never loses sight of Lucius no matter where they go. He speaks when he is spoken to and drops back whenever Lucius wants to talk to one of his own friends. His language is moderate and restrained, and he never answers a question without pausing for a moment to choose the most suitable words.

Demetrius is very learned, and Lucius remembers with shame how he once played a horrible game with his friends, asking him questions and threatening to have him beaten for any lack of knowledge in his answers. In fact Demetrius was more than equal to the boys, but Flavius found out what was going on and gave Lucius a taste of what he was offering to do to Demetrius.

Demetrius never held anything against him, however. He has explained often that a truly balanced man should be able to disregard everything outside his own mind, and that even slavery, imprisonment, torture or death can have no hold over him if he achieves a proper state of detachment. He tries, but not very hard, to convert Lucius to this idea. Perhaps he knows it is not much use. Lucius believes in being well-fed and well-exercised, and in taking advantage of every chance he gets for a little fun. This is the Italian way, and is after all very pleasant.

On their way they catch up with Flavius' litter. He is carried by four Syrian slaves, while four more walk before and behind him. This is a fairly modest escort compared with the one that accompanied him to the Forum in the morning. Then a small army of his clients followed him— building contractors, tradesmen, army officers, soldiers and scholars, so that he was admired by all the people for his importance and popularity. Flavius really knows all these people well, and believes that a truly great man can be familiar with everyone, without losing his dignity.

He looks rather tired now, but also rather contented, and as Lucius walks along beside the litter he tells him about the

morning's work. He has spent quite a long time with Marcus, his banker and agent, and he says that two of his deals have turned out better than he had expected. Since most of his success hinges on getting a quiet hint about the right moment to buy, he gives no details. His slaves have been with him for years, but still it would be a miracle if at least one of them were not being paid by another rich man to listen and repeat anything profitable in his conversation.

At the house, Flavius climbs out of the litter and he and Lucius go in together.

By this time, Julia has come back from the Forum and is resting in her room. She is feeling the heat, because of her heavy silk clothes, and besides the business of making her will was depressing. Her dressing-woman fusses over her, but this only annoys Julia. She sends for Cornelia, who is glad to get away from the embroidery that she was working at. Julia lies back on her bed and lets Cornelia fan her with her huge fan of dyed feathers, while she shows off her new cameo. Cornelia admires it very much. It is as big as the palm of her hand, so that the perfection of the carving can be clearly seen. The heavy gold setting is beautifully worked.

Since the middle of the morning the shutters have been closed against the blistering sun. The only light comes through the chinks and the people stay inside like mice when the cat is around. Cornelia hates to be shut in like this but there is no help for it until the whole family moves out to Tusculum for the summer. She is looking forward to this, not only because it will be cooler but because she will have much more freedom there.

Flavius' villa in Tusculum is said to be one of the finest in that area, which is saying a great deal. Many rich Romans have summer villas in the Alban hills and they compete with each other in furnishings and in the entertainment they offer their friends. Flavius' villa has been in the family for generations. There is nothing ostentatious about it. He agrees with

27

the poet Horace that it's a poor house where the valuables unseen and unthought of do not exceed all those that are on show. This idea, together with his notion that all Romans are men of the soil, tends to make the house rather bare for some tastes, but this is one of the reasons why it is so pleasant in summer. It has big wide terraces decorated with trees growing in pots, and flowering creepers against the outer walls. Always when the family goes out there in June, the jasmine is in full flower, and the scent of it sweetens the air, especially in the evening. The view from the terraces is beautiful, little hills covered with olive trees and vines. Flocks of sheep move among the trees, while their shepherds sit in a shady place, watching them.

Best of all is the fact that there are no mosquitoes in Tusculum. The nearest river is miles away and there are no standing ponds where they can breed. The garden fountains keep the water moving day and night, because a local stream has been partly diverted to run through them. This was done by the original builder of the house and it is said that the fountains have never ceased to play since they were first put in motion three hundred years ago.

The garden paths are hedged with box and rosemary, and there are fig and mulberry trees to give shade. Stone seats are set under the trees, and here and there marble busts of Roman scholars are let into niches in the walls.

Flavius is very proud of his library, and rightly so. It is well known, and scholars come from as far away as Greece to read his manuscripts.

Cornelia listens to the scholars' discussions whenever she can. She has no patience with the idea that a girl need not be educated, and she envies Lucius his opportunities for learning things that she has to search out for herself. Her mother has explained carefully to her that there is no harm in a Roman woman being educated, provided that she can order her household perfectly at the same time, but she has also warned her that many men, even intellectual ones, would think twice before marrying a woman who has been educated beyond the domestic arts. It is thought that an educated woman is likely to neglect her family, and will probably be such a bad housekeeper that after a while her husband will divorce her.

The awful warning is Clodia, to whom Catullus addressed so many poems. She behaved badly in almost everything, Cornelia has been told, and so did Sempronia, whose son Brutus was one of Julius Caesar's assassins. Sempronia could play and dance more elegantly than an honest woman should, Julia said, and she also ran up bills and conspired in a murder.

Cornelia does not agree that these faults were caused by education, but she is careful not to say so. What she has learned is that women must buy the right to use their brains by first showing that they are highly efficient in their everyday work. She has an example of an educated woman of good sense, to balance the example of Clodia. This is a namesake of her own, Pompey's wife Cornelia, who was highly educated, played the lute well and understood geometry and philosophy, which were usually thought to be beyond the comprehension of women.

When Julia has cooled off, it is time for the whole family to assemble for luncheon. This meal is really a hearty snack, and there is no ceremony about it. No one sits or lies down, and each person helps himself to whatever he fancies. There is bread and cold meat, salad and fruit, and wine to drink. There are also cheeses made of sheep's milk from the farm at Tusculum and Flavius makes his meal only of these. His doctor has warned him about putting on weight and as there will be a banquet in the evening he thinks it prudent to hold off at lunchtime.

Lucius has some of everything and still feels only half full. Cornelia likes the cold meat and fruit, but since she saw the cheese being made in the dairy in Tusculum she has not been able to bring herself to eat it. The dairy was scrubbed clean, but the shepherd who brought in the milk looked as if he had not washed since the day he was born.

After luncheon, everyone has a sleep. The house slaves lie down on the cool marble of the entrance hall and the dining-room, the cooks lie in the shade of a tree that grows in the yard by the kitchen door, and the members of the family go to their rooms. The wine has made everyone drowsy, and very soon the whole house is perfectly still.

An hour later, Lucius is up and about again. The rest of the family is still asleep and he has chosen this quiet time specially to go down to the stables and see how his horses are getting on. He owns three, and each one has a slave of its own to look after it. Though Lucius is interested in the law and knows it will be a fine thing to be a Senator, still he finds that this hour that he spends with the horses is the most real part of the day. He feels more at home with Aurelius the jockey than he does with Gaius. He is a little ashamed of this feeling, which does not become a Roman gentleman, but on the other hand he knows that some others of his own social class feel the same.

Aurelius is a slave whose father and grandfather worked in the family stables. He has a genius for horses. They seem to know him, and he always greets them before he looks at the people, when he comes into the stables. Already he has won several dozen races, and he rides with such ease that Lucius fears his father will sell him for a high price to one of the chariot-racing factions. At the last race, Aurelius lay down on the back of his horse in full gallop; then he stood up, then knelt with one hand held up to acknowledge the delighted yells of the crowd. Afterwards Lucius saw his father talking to the manager of the Greens, who have their big stables down by the river. Aurelius would probably be very glad to go to them, knowing that they would certainly free him soon, as a reward for making them so much money.

No private person could compete with the arrangements

that the factions have at their stables. They have stable-boys, grooms and trainers, saddlers, tailors to make coverings for the horses and coloured tunics and leggings for the charioteers, veterinary surgeons to look after the horses' health, watchmen for their safety, and even a crowd of professional applauders, like those employed by the lawyers, to cheer for their teams on the day of the races. When it comes to getting a good charioteer, they compete with each other in the price they will pay for him, rather as good soccer players are bought by clubs in our day.

There are four main factions, each known by the colours that the charioteers wear: the Reds, the Blues, the Greens and the Whites. At the races, there are events for various teams: for chariots drawn by two, three or four horses. Sometimes chariots are drawn by six, eight or ten horses but the biga races, with two horses, are the most popular because they are the fastest.

Race days are tremendous events. Lucius would not miss one for anything. The Great Circus, which has recently been enlarged still more, is just at the foot of the Aventine Hill where his family lives. It is six hundred and fifty yards long and more than two hundred yards wide. Two hundred and sixty thousand people can watch the races, from tiers of wooden seats placed on the slope of the Aventine Hill at one side and the Palatine Hill at the other. As the Emperor has his palace up there, he has a special royal box for himself and his family, which he can enter without leaving his own garden. He nearly always comes. Indeed, the Romans are none too pleased if he stays away, no matter how busy he is.

The race-track itself is covered in fine silvery sand. It is curved to form a semi-circle at both ends. A sort of embankment runs along the middle of the track, and on top of it there are seven big wooden eggs alternated with seven bronze dolphins. As each of the seven laps of the race is completed, one of the eggs is moved aside and one of the dolphins is turned around. In the centre is an obelisk brought from Egypt.

At one end of the Circus there are twelve boxes where the horses wait, harnessed to the chariots, to begin the race. Above them is the tribune where the judge who presides over the games sits with his retinue, all dressed in magnificent robes. When the race is to begin, the judge lets a white handkerchief fall from his box, the rope stretched in front of the horses is dropped and they're off.

The crowd shrieks and yells and dances up and down, everyone cheering for the team he has backed. There can be as many as twelve teams. The start is fairly easy, when they sail down the long straight, the charioteer proudly standing, wearing his helmet and a tunic the colour of his faction. The reins of all the horses are tied around his waist and he carries a dagger in his hand to cut them if there is an accident. Rounding the curves at either end of the track is the most dangerous part of the business. There is a wooden post which he must avoid. At the same time he must not crash into the other chariots which are attempting to pass, and whose charioteers will try to force him against the opponent on his other side.

The two middle horses are harnessed to the central shaft but the outside pairs are attached only with traces so that they are running loose. On them depends the charioteer's fate at the turns. Luckily the horses are not only well-trained but highly intelligent. They don't want to end up in a mass of flailing hooves and splintered wood, so they take care to avoid the teams at either side of them. What they think of the whole affair is a complete secret, but they certainly play their part as if they enjoy it. Most of the horses are Spanish, five years old or more, and they have been training for this kind of racing from the age of three.

There are other entertainments in the Great Circus—fights between gladiators, or between a gladiator and a wild animal, are the most popular, but these are often held at the Colosseum because the Great Circus is too big to give everyone a good view. Pompey once brought twenty African elephants there but they went so wild when they were prodded by the gladiators that no one has had the nerve to do it since. Lions and leopards are the most usual animals nowadays. Lucius and his friends enjoy the gladiator fights especially, as it gives them some of the feeling of excitement that they are looking forward to when they go to the wars.

None of the boys find the spectacle disgusting, though people like Pliny often write and speak against the practice. Lucius thinks Pliny has a right to do this as he is a philosopher as well as a politician, and philosophers may be as odd as they please—no one need take any notice of them—but his father gets quite angry about it. Talk like this could upset the whole Roman way of life, he says. The prospect of the Circus keeps the common people at their work from day to day. Who knows how long the present world would last if they had time to think about their condition? Before you could say "knife" they would be plotting revolution.

Since he owns Aurelius and three horses, Lucius' main interest is in the races. However, he would not think of riding in them himself. That is the business of a slave. Lucius rides very well, and his father has a year-old stallion in training for him to take to the wars, whenever he is ready to go. His life will depend to a large extent on that horse and on his own skill as a rider.

Cornelia enjoys the races too, but for different reasons. Going there is her best occasion for dressing up, and lately she has even been allowed to paint her face, though not as much as her mother does. She is almost full-grown, and she loves to be gazed at in admiration by the young men of patrician families.

Her mother has made it plain that it is not too early to be looked over as a prospective wife. Even Emperors have been

33

known to divorce their middle-aged wives when their eyes lit on a beautiful young girl, all got up for the races or a holiday or a religious festival.

It is more likely, however, that Cornelia will be married to the son of one of her father's colleagues, or even to a Senator of her father's generation. If this happens, she would like him not to be too old and bald, not so much for any personal reason as because her friends would certainly laugh at her. The older sister of one of her friends was bestowed at eighteen on a very rich Senator of sixty, and though she tries to put a

good face on it, one can see that she finds her new life dull.

Several of Cornelia's friends have been engaged to be married for years, from the age of ten or eleven. Cornelia's cousin Marcia was married a short time ago, when she was fourteen, and Cornelia was very much impressed with the wedding ceremony. Marcia's and Cornelia's fathers are brothers, so the whole family was at the wedding.

First Marcia put on her wedding dress, and dedicated her old palla and her dolls to the family god. Then she put on a red veil and a woollen belt fastened with a special knot. The priest sacrificed a sheep, and spent some time examining its intestines for portents. When the priest said that the future looked bright for the young pair, Marcia's great-aunt who was directing the ceremonies told them to join their right hands. Another sheep was sacrificed and then the wedding feast began.

In the evening, the wedding procession left Marcia's house for her new husband's home. A boy walked in front carrying a torch, and two others held the bride by a hand each. These boys had to be sons of parents who were both living. There was an escort of flute-players as well, and at her husband's house Marcia was given oil and fat to smear on the doorposts, and a piece of woollen cloth to tie around each. Then her husband carried her over the threshold. Some say that this is done to commemorate the foundation of Rome, when the Roman men could get no women to marry, so they invited their neighbours the Sabines to a feast and at the height of the fun seized a Sabine woman each and carried her home. Though the method of acquiring a wife was rough, the women said that Roman men made excellent husbands and they decided to stay.

At the races, what amuses Cornelia most is watching the clothes of the fashionable women. Some of these are quite extraordinary and they seem to be wearing all their jewels at once. In Julius Caesar's time there was a law against dressing too grandly but it has lapsed, and some of the women look like walking jewellers' shops. Even the horses have strings of pearls threaded into their manes and tails.

The President of the games is the finest sight of all, with a scarlet tunic and an embroidered toga. He has an ivory baton in his hand, with an eagle made of gold on top, and a wreath of golden leaves on his head, so heavy that a slave has to stand by to hold it in position.

The sun shines down on all this glitter and the great sweaty crowd yells and howls, so that Cornelia always comes home with a headache. However, she thinks it is well worth it and she looks forward to race days very much.

On this June afternoon, there are no races. When Lucius has had a good look at his horses and a chat with Aurelius, he decides to go to the baths. This is where he will meet all his friends. His father and mother and Cornelia will do the same, for Romans of all ages are encouraged to believe that a certain amount of regular exercise is essential to keeping mind and body in a state of health.

This subject of health is a favourite one with Pliny. His latest example is an old man called Vestricius Spurinna, who is seventy-eight years old but does not look it, and whose sight and hearing are still perfect. On Pliny's last visit to Flavius' house he described how this man spent his day. Spurinna is very rich, or he would not be able to live so well. Lucius thought that his life sounded a bit dull, but Pliny said that when a man is old, business is unseasonable and ambition would be indecent, so a calm regular life is entirely suitable.

Spurinna lies in bed until eight o'clock, when he calls for his shoes and takes a three-mile walk. Then, if he has friends staying with him, he sits and chats with them for a while. If he is alone, he gets a slave to read to him. After that he has a rest, and more conversation and reading, and Pliny says that his conversation is often as educational as any book could be.

After this his chariot is brought around and he goes for a seven-mile drive with his wife, or any friend who happens to be staying with him. Somewhere along the way he gets out and walks a mile. When he reaches home again, he goes into his study and writes poetry, which he does very well in both Greek and Latin.

Like every rich man who lives in the country he has baths of his own in the house. At two o'clock in summer and at three in winter, he goes to the baths and undresses himself, and walks about naked in the sun if there is no wind. Then he plays ball with a slave or with his friends for a long time until he is in a good sweat, and finally he gets into the baths.

Naturally he feels tired after all this exercise, so he lies on his couch to wait for dinner, while someone reads to him and to his friends who have been at the baths with him. He eats well but simply, and no one complains of getting indigestion after one of his meals. One reason may be that everything is very leisurely, and though he sits on a long time after dinner sipping wine, he is such amusing company that the visitors are never bored.

Like Spurinna, Flavius has a bath in the house for the use of the family. However, on a warm summer's day like this, they all prefer to go to the public baths. At this time, in the year A.D. 110, men and women use the baths at the same time. There are separate baths which women may use if they wish, and in a later age there will be special hours for women and others for men, but just now mixed bathing is allowed.

There are hundreds of public baths in Rome. The one where Flavius and his family go is quite near their house on the Aventine Hill. It is rather new, as it was built by the present Emperor, but it is not the newest of all. Only last year the Emperor opened another one, much more magnificent, but since it is down near the Forum it is not so airy in summer.

The whole family sets out together, Cornelia and her mother in litters carried by slaves, while Lucius and Flavius walk alongside. Livia carries a bag containing the tights that Cornelia will wear in the exercise ground. Julia's dressing-woman is there too, and about twenty other slaves, including of course Demetrius, who walks beside Lucius. On the way he talks to Lucius about the Spartans, who were such wonderful atheletes and soldiers, and who established the tradition of games in Greece.

Lucius hardly listens. He hears it all every day on his way to the baths, and he knows it is Demetrius' way of saying that

38

the Greeks are better than the Romans. Lucius finds the Greek idea of games dull and over-refined, and he is tempted to point out to Demetrius that the cruder Romans are a lot more successful than the Greeks in conquering distant countries. However, he does not dare to say things like this to Demetrius in his father's hearing. Flavius is never tired of pointing out that while the Romans excel in physical strength and in war, the Greeks are mainly noted for their intellectual achievements. He would like Lucius to be a perfect mixture of intellectual and man of action, and he watches for any signs of a lack of respect for scholars.

Outside the baths, at either side of the entrance there is a row of little shops, but no trading is allowed inside. Flavius pays a very small entrance fee, a few asses (which are not donkeys but small Roman coins) for each member of the family, and they all go into the lovely garden beyond the entrance door.

At once, Lucius sees Gaius with some other boys, and he goes off to join them. Cornelia's litter is lowered to the ground beside her mother's and she gets out. The gardens are at their best. The weather only got really hot about ten days ago and the flowers and trees look fresh and shiny. Up here the air is delightful.

Hundreds of people of all classes are walking about, either taking the air and admiring the flowers or else going towards the buildings where the baths themselves are housed. These are in the middle of the park, and Cornelia always feels a sense of excitement as she reaches them with her parents and their retinue. Everything is so perfectly arranged there, one never gets bored, even though they come to the baths almost every day.

The buildings are shaped like the letter D, with the curve at the back. They are built of small flat bricks faced with marble, and are very dignified and imposing.

The dressing-rooms are just inside the entrance. Here Livia

helps Cornelia out of her palla and her underclothes, and into her tights. Cornelia loves the feeling of freedom they give her, so that she begins to prance up and down at once as if she were already in the exercise ground.

Julia's dressing-woman helps her into a light tunic, and Flavius' slave puts one on him also. Across the room they can see that Lucius has already been dressed by Demetrius in his tunic. They put the clothes into niches in the walls, and then they all go through the great halls to the exercise grounds.

The curved back of the building gives on to a cool covered walk, which you cross to reach the playing grounds. Beyond

that again there are sitting-rooms and libraries, and great halls where exhibitions of painting and sculpture are held.

In the exercise ground, families or groups of friends are playing games of different kinds, all of them very energetic. Some pairs are wrestling. These are quite naked. They have smeared themselves with oil and then covered themselves with sand, so that they look like stone statues that have suddenly taken to fighting. Both men and women play this game but Cornelia thinks it would be horrible to have to get so dirty first.

What she likes is to play a three-cornered ball game with

41

Livia and her mother. They form a triangle and throw the ball from one to the other, as fast and as unexpectedly as possible. They catch with one hand and throw with the other, and often pretend to throw in one direction but change at the last moment in the hope of catching out a different person.

The ball is made of cloth stuffed with feathers. If it falls, none of the players picks it up. That is the business of the slave who is standing by watching them.

Lucius and a crowd of other boys have started a ferocious game with a ball stuffed with sand. They fight each other for this ball, and when one has possession of it, the others all fall on him together and take it from him. One cannot go on too long with this. After a while they call to their slaves for swords and begin mock battles with a fencing post. They are all planning to get to the wars some day, and they attack the post as if it were a Parthian.

When Cornelia and her mother are tired of playing with the ball, Livia brings them a hoop each, and a little stick to roll it with. By the time they have run up and down the long sandy exercise ground several times after their hoops, they are beginning to sweat. Indeed, this begins rather too soon at this time of year. Cornelia prefers the winter when she can run and play for much longer. Now the sun is beating down and the hoops are going more slowly, and at last they come to a stop.

They go back into the bath-house. Flavius has been playing a game of handball with some other senators, against a wall specially built for the purpose. The Emperor has come in, and he joins in the game for a while. He is a simple, kindly man and a close friend of Flavius, who knows that he can always ask a favour of him.

Flavius leaves his own group now and joins his family. First they go back to the dressing-room and take off all their clothes. Then they go into the sweating-room. This is a hall which is lined with cubicles heated by steam pipes that run under the floor. They stay in the cubicles for a while, to continue the sweating process, which is considered very healthy.

Next they move into an adjoining room which is also very hot, but here there is a great basin of hot water in the middle of the room. The slaves take a dipper each and splash the hot water repeatedly over their masters, scraping their bodies all over between times with a specially made scraper called a strigil, rather as one grooms a horse.

All around them, other people are being tended in the same way. Anyone who is too poor to afford a slave has to ask a friend to scrape him, and he returns the same service. Rich and poor mix quite freely at the baths, though some can afford better treatment than others. For instance, anyone who pays an extra fee can use one of the small bathing-rooms off the main hall, if he wants to bath in private, or he can pay a masseur to rub him all over with oil.

When they feel clean and fresh after the scraping, they go back to the first hall, by the entrance, where the temperature is barely warm. Here they cool down gradually. When they have stopped sweating, they go into the last hall, where the cold bath is.

This bath is very big, so that a large number can bathe together, and there is a rule that no clothing of any kind is to be worn. The bath itself is open to the sky, but the surrounding space is covered in. Lucius swims from end to end of the bath, feeling wonderfully fresh and powerful. Cornelia delays in this bath too, but Flavius and Julia get out rather quickly and are rubbed down with towels by their slaves. Julia's dressing-woman tidies up her hair and sprinkles scent on her. Flavius' slave has scent for him too, but not too much. Flavius says that scent should only be used by a man to the amount necessary to conceal the natural smell of the body. Any more than that is unbecoming.

When Cornelia and Lucius get out of the cold bath, they

are rubbed down too, and then they all go to dress. There is still some daylight, so instead of going home at once they take a stroll through the gallery to see if there are any new statues. The Emperor is very modest and does not like statues of himself to be put up, but he has commissioned works from the best sculptors in white marble, portrait busts of eminent Romans and some groups of figures depicting well-known scenes from the history of Rome. Everywhere there are fountains. Water is plentiful in Italy, and there are plenty of clever engineers to make use of it. There are fountains carved with fish and boats and horses, and some plain round basins carved with leaves and surmounted by a simple statue of a god or goddess.

Strolling about, they come upon Flavius' business friend Marcus, standing outside the library. His son is in there, he says, but he prefers the fresh air outside to a musty old library.

Cornelia looks into the room. She likes Marcus' son Gallus, and on the few occasions when they have met he has talked to her seriously about the Greek philosophers. She sees him now, at the far end of the library, under the carved, domed, marble ceiling. He is talking to a Greek slave who has taken down one of the wooden chests from its niche in the wall and is getting him out a manuscript. Cornelia wonders which one it is, but her father has finished his talk with Marcus and they must move on.

The slaves bring litters, this time for Flavius too, and they all get in. Livia covers Cornelia with a woollen rug lest she might catch cold. Cornelia almost falls asleep as she is borne gently home.

At the house there is a great bustle going on. The marble pavements are all shining. The lamps are ready filled with oil, and though the banquet will not begin for more than an hour, two slaves are already standing by the door in case someone happens to come early. Flavius is pleased with this, and he goes into the house in good humour.

44

By now Lucius is wildly hungry. He gets Demetrius to sneak down to the kitchen and bring him a snack to keep him alive until dinner-time. His father would not approve of this. If he were to see Lucius so dependent on food, he would certainly discourse to him on the importance for a soldier of being able to live on his fat for a few days when necessary. In Pompey's great campaign against Mithridates, he says, when the Empire was extended greatly, no one was sure of three meals a day. Time enough to go hungry when he has to, Lucius thinks, and he guzzles a quail and some bread that one of the cooks gave to Demetrius for him.

No one will go hungry in Flavius' house tonight. He is very hospitable, and he spares no expense to ensure that his guests have the best that the Empire can provide. Still, he is no glutton, and his guests need not expect to be given so much at one meal that they will feel ill for days afterwards. This is ostentation, Flavius says, and neither does he believe in presenting the dishes in strange ways, giving them too much importance. Marcus does this, and Flavius has to suffer it in silence when he goes to dine with him. It shows a lack of confidence in himself, Flavius thinks, and he is always hoping that Marcus will learn something of how a Roman gentleman should behave, from the example of Flavius' house.

Tonight's party is not a very big one. There are twenty-seven in all, including Flavius and Julia, and each person must be provided with a reclining place on a couch. Lucius and Cornelia will eat sitting on stools beside their parents. Since Lucius is in theory a man, he should perhaps be given a reclining place too, but so far his father has not suggested it.

The dining-room in Flavius' house is very spacious, as it needs to be. Tonight there are three square tables rather near the walls. Three couches are set at each table, one at each of three sides, leaving the fourth side, which faces towards the room, free so that the meal can be easily served and so that the diners can see the entertainments. Three people can recline on each couch, and cushions are laid on them to mark the division of the places.

Flavius will have the middle place at the central table, and he has worked out in advance exactly where his guests will sit, in order of their importance.

The guest of honour tonight is a Pro-Consul who has just come back to Rome. He will be placed at Flavius' right hand side. Julia will have the place at Flavius' left, and beside her will be an eminent member of the College of Augurs. He must be treated with immense respect, and Flavius confides to Lucius his fears that these two great men will be jealous of each other.

However, as Flavius himself is likely to be appointed by the Emperor to some high office any day now, he does not expect that either of his guests will show their chagrin, if they feel it. Being a friend of the Emperor puts him in a very strong position.

Most of the guests are accompanied by a slave or a freedman of their own. For dining, they wear a special lightweight tunic, and they have brought some spare ones in case they want to change during the evening. This is thought a very proper thing to do, when one is hot and sweaty from eating.

In the entrance hall, the guests take off their shoes and the slaves wash their feet for them. Then they go in to meet Flavius and Julia, and lie down on the couches.

At once, house slaves come around with jugs of scented water and bowls. They pour the water over the guests' hands and wipe them dry with a towel. Then they place crowns of flowers on their heads and the meal can begin.

The table is laid with a linen cloth, and with knives and spoons. There are no forks, since no one has thought of such an idea yet, so people pick up their food with their fingers. This is a very convenient method, though it does mean that the slaves have to keep coming around with their jugs of water after each course.

Everyone has a table-napkin to keep the couch coverings clean, and people with small appetites have brought in napkins of their own as well, so that they can bring home in them anything they cannot finish. Flavius regards it as a compliment to his kitchen when he sees a guest place some prawns or pieces of chicken or fine bread in his napkin. He certainly does not think it unmannerly.

The first course is an hors d'oeuvre of eggs and tunny and shell-fish and mushrooms and other delicate vegetables, with small hot rolls of white bread. Next comes a dish of baked mullet and sole, and then some quails cooked in honey and wrapped in slices of smoked ham. After that there is a dish of lobsters with little fried, spiced vegetable marrows.

With each of these dishes there is a different wine, beginning with the white wine from Flavius' own vineyard in Tusculum. No one drinks the wine neat. This would be considered very coarse. The slaves bring the wine in jars and pour it into a huge bowl. Then they add one-third as much water, and serve it to the guests in little drinking bowls.

Now it is time for the two main courses, first wild boar and then a whole calf. They are accompanied by vegetables cooked in oil and spices, and are washed down with more wine, this time from the more distant parts of the Empire. One wine comes from Gaul and another from Spain.

At last Lucius feels he is getting enough to eat. Cornelia is astonished at the amount of food he can put away. She does not attempt to eat all she is offered but shares a dish with her mother if she likes the look of it.

Between each of the courses, while the tables are being cleared and the guests' hands washed, there is a short entertainment—a Spanish dancer with castanets, and a juggler, and a troupe of acrobats.

When the sixth course is finished, the tables are taken away and other, more ornamental ones are brought in for the dessert. This consists of a cake in the form of a pyramid, four feet high, surrounded by dried and fresh fruits of all kinds. The pyramid is composed of a pile of tiny cakes, all filled with custard, and the whole edifice is coated in sticky icing. By now the guests are all so full of food and wine that they are forgetting the formality of their behaviour when they arrived.

When she cannot stand another minute of the noise, Cornelia slips away to her room. It is cool and quiet there, and Livia is waiting for her, asleep on the mat by the bedside. She helps Cornelia into bed and blows out the lamp. Cornelia can hear the racket from the dining-room, and though she falls asleep almost at once, the shouts and yells of the guests disturb her from time to time. It is almost daylight before the last of them goes home and the house is quiet at last.

CHAPTER TWO

A Businessman's Family

Although Marcus is not a Senator like Flavius, he is a much richer man. Until three years ago he lived on the Quirinal Hill, on the ground floor of a huge block of flats. It was a convenient place to live, being near to all his business interests and contacts, but lately his affairs have prospered so much that he has felt the need to build himself a magnificent house. He has not moved very far away from the old one, and he is still in the business centre of the City, on the Esquiline Hill. However, he has a fine garden around his house, as befits a member of the Equestrian Order.

The only qualification for membership is to own a certain amount of money, and in fact Marcus owns many times the required amount.

Gallus, his son, likes the new house much better than the apartment in which they used to live. This is not only because it is furnished and decorated in the most expensive way, with polished pink marble pillars and tortoiseshell inlay and silver beds and tables. What Gallus likes is that there is space in plenty, great airy rooms and halls where one can be quiet, and gardens full of the twittering of birds and the splash of fountains.

So far Gallus has little interest in business. His mother was a gentle, quiet woman, the daughter of a patrician family who cared only for philosophy and poetry and cultivated company. Marcus had hoped that she would bring him some prestige and so she did. But he was bored with her company and she always made him feel small, though she had no wish to do so. She died young, and Marcus' present wife Aemilia is a healthy, noisy woman, much more to his taste. She is a fine housekeeper, and she is as good to Gallus and his sister Valeria as she knows how. She has two children of her own but she is not in the least jealous about getting them precedence over the older family.

On this fine morning Gallus wakes up earlier than usual. The last thought in his mind before he fell asleep was of some Greek poetry which he had been trying to translate into Latin. He calls out to his slave to bring the manuscript and read it to him while he is dressing. Gallus is only fifteen but he has already gone a long way towards fitting himself to be a poet. Translating Latin into Greek and Greek into Latin, both in prose and verse, is considered a most useful exercise. His tutor Neocles, who is Greek of course, has great hopes of him.

Neocles is a freedman. He was bought at an auction when he was twenty, eleven years ago, and given complete charge of Gallus' education. He was chosen by Gallus' mother. She believed in Greek education, especially in Greek philosophy, and she directed Neocles exactly in how he was to educate her son. In her will she decreed that he was to be given his freedom but this did not mean that he had to leave the household. Marcus kept him in his service out of respect for his dead wife's wishes. Gallus has never been to a regular school but Neocles has given him an excellent course in literature and philosophy.

Marcus has no patience with Neocles and has not allowed him to educate his other children. He says that philosophy and literature only teach people to talk well, and then they forget that the most important duty of a Roman is to fight. All these Greek philosophers and doctors were captured by the Romans, and their learning did not save them. You can't think well and do well, he says. Besides, philosophers and literary men are always preaching sedition, trying to tyrannise over the country and undermine its ancient customs, and encouraging the citizens to break the law. If he had his way, there would not be a philosopher in the Empire.

Marcus distrusts all Greeks, in fact. This is awkward, at times, since the only doctors are Greeks, but if anyone gets sick Marcus claims that he is able to cure them. He has an idea that over-eating is the cause of all sickness, and indeed this is true of himself. When he hears of a slave or a member of the family being sick, he makes out a list of what they are to eat—certain vegetables and herbs, or the meat of a pigeon or a hare. He prescribes a roast thrush or a quail for special cases. If the patient recovers he boasts of his skill but if the person dies, Marcus blames the gods or says that the priests did not read the auguries correctly, when they examined the animals' entrails after the sacrifice. Indeed it is possible that Gallus' mother would be alive today if Marcus had called in a doctor to attend to her.

When Gallus is dressed, he passes through the crowd of his father's clients in the entrance hall. This morning they are all admiring Marcus' new water-clock which has been erected in the middle of the ornamental pool in the hall. It does not tell the time accurately but that does not matter since no one cares that much about punctuality. Every hour, more or less, its floats rise with the water, which is carefully controlled, until they reach a certain height. Then a whistle blows, the water runs out quickly through a vent and the float starts rising again. Who could care whether the whistle blows regularly?

Marcus is moving around among the clients, dropping a

word here and there, making appointments for later in the morning, getting little bits of information which will be useful to him in his various business ventures. Several of these are pretty dubious but Marcus always insists that once one is in business one cannot afford to be foolishly scrupulous.

One of his main activities is in building and house property of all kinds. His slaves work fast, both at pulling down old buildings and putting up new ones. Usually the pulling down part is easy. Marcus never buys a house in good condition. That is only for people who know no better. What he does is to wait until a house falls down or goes on fire, in the poorer quarter of the City. Then he goes along to the owner and offers a low cash price for the site and the rubble. The owner nearly always accepts, in his despair at seeing his property in ruins. Then Marcus sends around his slaves, who quickly run up a new building which will go on fire or fall down in a few years' time, but not before Marcus has trebled his outlay at the very least.

The houses that Marcus builds are four or five storeys high, and each floor is rented as a flat to a family. The ground floor is usually a shop or, if the frontage is long, two or three shops. Each shop has a tiny living-room, like a mouse's nest, tucked into the space between its low ceiling and the first floor, and underneath the flat above. The owner of the shop lives, eats and sleeps in that little space. There is even a flat under the roof, cold in winter and like an oven in summer, so the rent up there is lower.

One reason why the houses fall down is that the walls are not thick enough. There is an old law against making them thick, designed to save space and to prevent people from building fortresses in the City, in the days when houses were only two storeys high at most. Though the houses are much higher now, the old law still holds. Another reason why the houses fall down is that there are no proper foundations, and as the centre of Rome is the marshy land around the Tiber, after a while one wall sinks a little into the mud and quickly drags the whole building down with it. Then it is a question of whether it is better to be buried in the rubble on the ground floor or hurled down from the top. At the first rumble, everyone shoots out shrieking into the street to warn the neighbours of what is happening. To make it worse, sometimes there are earthquakes. Even in our day one can feel tiny earthquakes in Rome quite often, and buildings with poor foundations could not survive them.

The reason for the fires is that in winter the rooms are heated with little earthenware or metal pots of charcoal and lit with candles, or lamps with open wicks. The bedclothes or the wooden floors of the upper storeys catch fire and the whole building goes up in smoke.

There is a fire brigade in Rome which was founded by Julius Caesar when he set up the police force. In the provinces there are no fire brigades, though several people have suggested to the Emperor that a band of men could be kept standing by in every city, waiting for a call to put out a fire, with special equipment of the kind that the Romans take to the wars. The present Emperor does not like the idea at all. He says that the firemen would quickly form themselves into a guild and would soon become a political association. He thinks it would be better for the householders to keep handy means of putting out fires, and to call in their neighbours if necessary.

The inefficiency of the Rome fire brigade suits Marcus. There is a big fire in the City every week, and he would not do half so well if they were extinguished early on.

This morning, when Marcus is ready to go out, Gallus goes with him and his retinue. Gallus, like Lucius, put on his man's toga this year. One or two of his friends are still wearing the purple-bordered toga of a boy, and they will have to wear it until their fathers consider that they are old enough to be treated like men. Some of his father's clients have brought their sons with them, and Gallus walks with them.

Marcus is carried in a litter, not because he is too weak to walk but because it seems to him more dignified. He is putting on weight and should take more exercise, but like many businessmen in our own day, he thinks that this would be a shocking waste of time. Besides, he wants to be able to duck back out of sight if he sees someone he wants to avoid. The litter has silk curtains embroidered with gold. It stands on four legs and has a pole fore and aft for carrying it. Two slaves could easily carry it but Marcus always has at least eight, for show.

Not all of Marcus' businesses are shady. In the warehouses in the city, he stores the goods that he imports from the East. Julia's fine silk dresses are all made from his silk and cotton. The spices used in Roman cooking are brought to him from India, on mule-back, by the route opened up by Alexander the Great's Greek army four hundred years ago. He buys gold and jewellery in India too, and ivory from Africa, where the elephants are so plentiful as to be a nuisance.

Nearer home, Marcus buys wool, which is a very profitable business indeed. Everyone wears it in the form of the toga, which is compulsory dress for Roman citizens. Mattresses are stuffed with wool and bed-coverings and rugs are made of it. Wool-buying was the main business of the unfortunate commerical town of Pompeii, which disappeared after the eruption of Vesuvius thirty-one years ago.

The Italians do not make fine woollen goods. Their cloth and their floor rugs are not as delicate as those imported from India, but Marcus rightly believes that there is more money to be made out of rough goods commonly used than out of luxury articles that will be too well cared for.

The crowd that goes with Marcus is much bigger than the one that accompanied Flavius to the Forum. A great many of his business associates are there and it is well known that he will resent it if they don't come often. Marcus was elected Tribune of the people once. This meant that he was a magistrate, and though he liked the importance it gave him, he found that it took up too much time. He did not seek re-election but he has kept his importance by lending money to the Government for foreign wars, and by collecting taxes from distant provinces. This is a safer activity. Tribunes and Consuls and Senators can find themselves in hot water over-night, whereas Marcus can warn his tax-collectors if an inspection is going to be carried out. He can cover up a great many of his crooked dealings before the envoys arrive from Rome.

What Marcus would really like is to be elected to the College of Augurs. This is a life appointment and carries great prestige. The duties could be performed by a child— deducing whether or not an undertaking will be a success from things like the flight of birds or the condition of the sacrificial animal's entrails. The priests do all the actual work, keeping a supply of animals and birds and killing them when the time comes. In interpreting, one guess is as good as another, often enough, and there are many simple rules which are easily followed. For instance, if the slaughtered chicken is found to have only one kidney, you advise the general against setting out for the wars that day. You never try to tell him what will happen if he goes.

Marcus has no belief in this kind of jiggery-pokery and would not dream of being guided by it in his business affairs, but he knows that it is a strong Roman tradition and as such must be continued.

Gallus cannot help admiring his father's energy and business acumen but he is not sure that he would like to do business in that way. Besides, his father is so rich that Gallus does not have to devote his energies to business. How better can Marcus' money be employed than in contributing to the culture of a Roman citizen?

Marcus encourages Gallus' intellectual tendencies, but with some doubt, since he does not understand how anyone could content himself with mere words when there is so much to be done. One reason why he likes his son to be a poet is that he feels rather lowered by the fact that his own grandfather was a slave who got on in the world. He was the steward of Flavius' grandfather who was twice elected Consul and was otherwise a very important man. Naturally the steward used his opportunities to make himself rich by taking bribes and by stealing judiciously from his master, so that when he was freed his son could start in business with a large capital.

Marcus knows that people have a horribly long memory for this kind of thing. He knows that his reputation improved when he married Gallus' mother but nevertheless he is always uncomfortable in the company of people like Pliny who look down their aristocratic noses at him. He knows they think him an utter vulgarian and he means to improve himself some day when he has time, but not yet. Pliny is himself a member of the College of Augurs and would have to sing rather smaller if the Emperor appointed Marcus too.

At the Forum, Gallus and his tutor separate from the rest of the party. Marcus is going on to Flavius' house. He is a client of Flavius and must pay him a visit every morning. He does not at all regard this as a waste of time. Flavius is his protector, if he ever needs one. He will give him legal advice and defend him in court if necessary. He is not allowed to take a fee for this but he expects Marcus to help him in his business affairs. This is no burden, because though Flavius acts so high and mighty he has a good nose for business and he deals fairly. For instance, last year Marcus bought the grapes from Flavius' farm in Tusculum to make wine. He bought them early in the season and afterwards a disease attacked the vines and reduced the value of the wine. Flavius actually gave back one tenth of the price he had been paid, though he could easily have said: "Let the buyer beware". There is a kind of old-fashioned innocence about Flavius that Marcus can't help admiring, and he tries not to cheat him too much in any of the business affairs that he manages for him. Besides, it's probably better to be on the safe side of a man who was Pro-Consul in Gaul for a while. Stories about Flavius circulate in Rome still, suggesting that he is not quite the innocent he makes himself out to be.

When his father has gone on, Gallus goes straight to the barber shop. Gallus has good, strong, dark hair which grows fast. Now he has to have a shave most days. His beard began to grow when he was thirteen and he kept it until last year. It was a bit on the furry side and made him feel silly, so he was glad when the time came to deposit it. It was a special ceremony, at the same time as he put on the man's toga. The house barber shaved off the beard, and a painful process it was, and put the hairs into a little gold box which Gallus himself placed among the household gods in the family chapel.

Gallus could go to be shaved by the house barber every day if he liked. His father owns more than a thousand slaves. Naturally he can afford to keep a barber among them but Gallus prefers to go to the public barber shop for a number of reasons. One is that the house barber is always too busy to give him time to explain what he wants. Marcus likes all the slaves to look neat and well-shaven but he grudges the money to send them down the town to a street-corner barber. This means that the house barber and his assistants are snowed under with customers every morning. The only one that gets proper attention is Marcus himself. This is natural, since he could have the whole lot of them hanged if he did not like his haircut.

Another reason why Gallus prefers not to have his hair and beard done at home is that the house barber is very old-fashioned. He gives everyone the same short-back-and-sides that Marcus likes. In the Forum there is a barber who is much

57

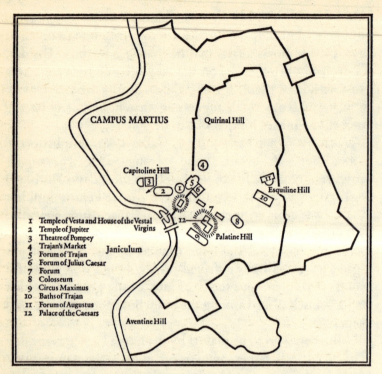

CAMPUS MARTIUS

Quirinal Hill

Capitoline Hill

Esquiline Hill

1   Temple of Vesta and House of the Vestal
      Virgins
2   Temple of Jupiter
3   Theatre of Pompey
4   Trajan's Market
5   Forum of Trajan
6   Forum of Julius Caesar
7   Forum
8   Colosseum
9   Circus Maximus
10 Baths of Trajan
11 Forum of Augustus
12 Palace of the Caesars

Janiculum

Palatine Hill

Aventine Hill

Rome in the time of Trajan

more enterprising. He does curls in complicated ways, making
the whole head look bigger. Perhaps his customers believe
in the saying of Lycurgus the Spartan that a fine head of hair
lends beauty to a good face and terror to an ugly one.
Whatever the reason, all the young men feel in a certain
sense supported by the volume of their hair when they leave
his shop.

Gallus has to wait for a while when he arrives. He does not
mind this as a number of his friends are there already and they
have plenty to say to each other. They sit on benches in the
shade of the awning outside the shop, chatting to each other
while they wait their turn, and watching the progress of the

customer on the central stool. He is swathed in a linen cloth and the chief barber is moving carefully around him, trimming his hair with a murderous-looking pair of iron scissors. These are so blunt and ill-balanced that they tug the hair painfully. The barber is as careful as he can be, but he is not too worried. He is a Roman citizen and he knows that his customer will think twice before stabbing him to death in revenge for an extra-strong tweak, as he would possibly do to a slave.

When he has trimmed the hair, one of the assistants hands the barber the metal tongs which he has been heating up in a little charcoal fire in the corner. With these the hair is arranged in a pile of curls. The beard has already been shaved and now another assistant comes forward and rubs the customer's cheeks with a special salve designed to cover the scars made by the daily razor. He gums a little circle of cloth over the worst ones. Then he gets out a pot of scented paste and puts some behind the customer's ears. The scent is so strong that the whole shop reeks with it.

The customer is a middle-aged man who was probably handsome enough once. Now he stands up and turns like a peacock in front of one of the mirrors that hang on the wall. He is watching for a sign of grey hairs but the dye he had put on last week is still holding its own. When he is satisfied he pays the barber and sails out of the shop with his chin in the air. The young people wait until he is well out of sight before bursting into giggles. The barber says nothing but lifts his shoulders and turns out his hands in a gesture that means a dozen things.

Now it is the turn of Octavius, one of the boys. The barber lets one of his assistants have a go at him and soon his shrieks of agony resound through the shop. No soap is used, only water, and the razor is incapable of being sharpened. Listening to the howls of his friend, Gallus decides to let his beard grow again. He will keep it trimmed and have the part

around his mouth shaved sometimes. This should be a less
painful affair than the daily shave which has lately become a
nightmare.

"So you are going into mourning?" the barber says
ironically when Gallus tells him that he only wants to have
his hair curled in future. For a long time, growing a beard has
been a sign of mourning.

"No," says Gallus. "I'm changing the fashion."

The barber does not like this but he can do nothing about
it. He knows it is what the Emperor wears that decides the
fashion and the Emperor has the sense to be clean-shaven, so
far at least. In any case this barber need not care what happens.
He has made such a huge fortune that he could retire for life,
if he wished.

In fact the next Emperor will fancy a beard, so the barbers will be put out of business, but at the moment it is one of the most flourishing trades in Rome.

All this time, Gallus' tutor Neocles has been standing apart with the other tutors, who are mostly slaves. One can tell this at a glance by the ring of lead that they wear on one finger. Some are freedmen who have remained at the only work they know. A slave who has been freed is not much better off than he was before, and he does not think it beneath him to keep up friendships with men who are still slaves.

Neocles likes this daily opportunity of some conversation with cultivated Greeks. He is lucky in having a responsive pupil. Most of the tutors have boys who care for nothing but parties and late nights, and whose only ambition is to go to war and make a name and a fortune for themselves.

In fact Gallus will have to go to war too, as his father insists on it. When he is seventeen he will have to serve in one campaign—no one doubts that there will be a campaign to serve in—so that he will be in line to be made a provincial governor some day. A man who has never served in the army cannot hope for such an appointment. For the same reason, Marcus has apprenticed Gallus to a well-known lawyer named Priscus, who will see to it that he has plenty of practice in the art of oratory. There is no fear that Gallus will be turned into a mere windbag, since Priscus believes that eloquence without wisdom is dangerous and that a man's first duty is to have something worth saying. After that he can consider how best to say it.

At the moment Gallus' main interest in the art of public speaking comes from the fact that he loves to read his own poems aloud in the Forum. Almost every day he goes to hear the poets, and some read so badly that he is determined not to make such a spectacle of himself when his own turn comes.

Poetry readings are very popular in Rome. They are held in private houses to audiences of connoisseurs, very dignified and grand, and also in the open air of the Forum or the baths, wherever the poet can find a handy flight of steps to stand on and a group of listeners to gaze up at him.

Gallus is intelligent enough to see that these readings are a poor way to bring one's work before the public. However, he finds them useful at his present stage, since he learns a great deal about the quality of his verses by speaking them aloud. Often he rejects a poem that he has read and decides not to have it copied at all. If he thinks well of it after he has read it, he puts it aside in the collection he is making. When he has enough of them, he hopes to bring them to one of the publishers who have their shops in various parts of the Forum. Priscus, his preceptor, is very friendly with Tryphon and has promised to recommend him. Tryphon may ask him to pay for the publication but if he does this, it will mean that he does not think much of the poems. He will not think that Gallus is too young to have his work considered. Quite a few famous writers made a start at fifteen or sixteen years old.

The publishers keep teams of highly-trained slaves who make copies of the works on papyrus. This is a kind of reed imported from Egypt. They write on one side of the paper only and stain the other side yellow. When the work has all been copied, the sheets are stuck together side by side in a continuous long piece, and then rolled up on to a short stick. The two ends of the stick are finished off with decorated wooden balls. To read the book, you begin to unroll it from the right-hand side, so that you read from right to left.

Books in a library are kept in a parchment case, with the name written on a piece of papyrus pasted on to the back. Since Julius Caesar opened the first public library in Rome, other rulers have followed suit and it is quite usual now to have a public library in every important city in the Empire. Besides, there are all the private libraries of the rich people, who will be sure to pass the word along if Gallus' work pleases them.

Already some of his poems have attracted notice, especially his short satires on Roman life. Neocles has a friend who is a slave in Pliny's house. He is a Greek too, and Pliny loves to have him take part in the learned discussions he has with his friends in the evenings. This friend says that the great man commended for punch and brevity of expression a poem which he heard Gallus read at the baths on the Campus Martius. It was a satire on the meaningless love poetry that Gallus hears so often and Pliny was so much amused by it that he remembered parts of it even after one hearing.

This morning a crowd has gathered around a tall, thin man who is standing on the steps of the Basilica Julia. Neocles takes Gallus' arm and guides him over to listen.

"Do you know him?" he asks.

"No," Gallus says. "But he looks over-anxious. He'll make his audience feel the same."

"Quite true," says Neocles. "He's a third-rate lawyer who suspects that he will never be a huge success, so he's leaving no stone unturned in his efforts to do all the things that the successful ones do. He started this only when he heard that Pliny sometimes polishes up a court speech and reads it aloud. Pliny's speech would be a thousand times better to begin with, and of course he would never come out and read it in public. He would know that this kind of thing is only for connoisseurs, so he just invites a few friends to his own house.

"In fact he had quite an argument with his friends on the question of repeating a speech as a recitation at all. They said that history or tragedy or lyric poetry was suitable for public recitation but not speeches which have been made already in their proper place. Pliny disagreed; he said that history is written to record truth, and tragedy should be played on the stage, and lyric poetry should be accompanied by the lyre, yet all these are recited in public. Besides, he said, all new things are suspect, and yet they must be introduced from time to time. His friends had to admit that the fact that it had never been done was not a good reason for not doing it now. And of course they think so highly of Pliny that they don't mind what he does."

Gallus agrees that Pliny is the greatest living Roman.

"As for that ass up there on the steps," Neocles goes on, "what he doesn't know is that anything that Pliny writes is literature. It's worth reciting. If this poor fellow were to talk from today until next week, he could never produce anything as neat and as full as Pliny does. Listen to him piling up adjectives and poking in long clauses where they only cause confusion. You would think he had never learned even the elements of grammar."

Gallus cannot help being sorry for the unfortunate lawyer and yet he is disgusted at the sight of his friends and relations cheering his miserable efforts. Immediately it occurs to Gallus to make a poem on this subject, that where natural talents are not enough to advance a man in the intellectual professions, the cheers and applause of his friends are doubly necessary. Family solidarity demands that deficiencies of the head be made up by the tongues and the palms of even the most remote cousins. He starts to work it out as he and Neocles walk on.

He will not mention the poem to Neocles until he has made the first draft of it, lest Neocles might urge him to write it in Greek. Though nowadays everyone who wants to do so writes in Latin, still Greek is thought by many people to be the superior language. This is not surprising, since most philosophy is written in Greek. Gallus intends to study in Athens some day but at present he feels more at home in his mother tongue. He knows that he must be able to write in both languages but one of his ambitions is to write so well in Latin that everyone will recognise that language as the equal of Greek.

Though Neocles' main concern is to cultivate Gallus' mind, he also encourages him to take part in athletics of all kinds. He has taught him to see that the so-called sports of the Amphitheatre are barbaric and to appreciate the cult of the body for its own sake. Most mornings, Gallus goes to the Campus Martius by the river, to practise various athletics for an hour—running, boxing and throwing the discus and the javelin. Gallus finds that this kind of exercise clears his head and gives him a sense of well-being, so that he feels more alert for the rest of the day. Besides, he enjoys the company of the other boys he meets there. All of them despise the popular and disgusting entertainment offered in the Amphitheatres and see their own type of sport as the only decent alternative.

Not all the intellectuals agree with them. Some say that the Greek-style games are unmanly and should be abolished. Even Pliny thinks they are a scandal and have a bad effect on Roman morals. The Greek gymnastics are performed in the nude, and those who object to them say that the attitudes of the athletes are different from those of the people who practise athletics at the baths.

The present Emperor rather encourages Greek games, in the hope that they will become popular and oust the gladiators and wild beasts as entertainment for the mass of the people. However, most people find them dull and seem to prefer the excitement of seeing people being killed in the arena.

Gallus has been to some shows in the Colosseum and found them quite horrifying. In fact he was so shocked that he has not been able to think clearly since then about what he saw. Perhaps because of his own ancestry, he cannot see the mass of the people as merely ignorant, to be kept quiet with any form of entertainment that they fancy. The Emperor's efforts to discourage the brutalities of the arena are not half strong enough, Gallus thinks. They should simply be stopped altogether, by a decree of the Emperor, and if a strong enough one ever comes along, perhaps he will do this. In fact two hundred years must pass before Rome is freed of these horrors by Constantine, the first Christian Emperor, but Gallus can see no prospect of anything so enlightened coming about.

His friends often go to the Colosseum and see no harm in the spectacle of a man fighting another man or an animal to the death. They say that the sight of such bravery is very good for the audience, and will make them brave in battle. No one in their senses would care about the animals, and the men were condemned anyway. Surely one can't be expected to sympathise with traitors and murderers and bandits? The people are often asked if they wish to spare the life of one of these criminals and the yell they give in favour of his death surely proves that they are very patriotic and care for the maintenance of law and order. And the gladiators are sometimes useful for training expert swordsmen for the army. Besides, even in the arena they have a sporting chance because if the people are impressed by a gladiator's bravery they may yell that he should be spared. This surely proves that the people have a say in how the Empire is governed.

Gallus thinks it proves that they are a bloodthirsty mob of ignoramuses, and he can see that the Emperor makes use of them and flatters them when he wants to get rid of someone. The present Emperor, Trajan, is a rather humane man, but even he does not feel able to put an end to a sport which keeps the Roman citizens out of harm's way most afternoons. At least they can't plot sedition at the Amphitheatre. There is too much noise, and the tradition is all against it. Afterwards everyone hurries home to supper because no eating is allowed in the Amphitheatre. By the time supper is over, they are too tired to do anything except go to bed.

While Gallus and Neocles are strolling around the Forum, Valeria has stayed quietly at home. Like Cornelia, she has her own slave who sleeps on a mat on her bedroom floor. She is a Greek girl but Valeria has named her Tullia.

Tullia does all the things for Valeria that Livia does for

Cornelia but as well as that she is a very well-educated girl. Her father was a philosopher who was killed in a minor war in Greece only four years ago. Tullia was brought to Rome and put up for sale. When Marcus bought her for Valeria, he knew only that she could sing and play the lyre. If he had known that she was also well educated in philosophy and Greek literature, he would probably have left her there.

Gallus has given Tullia books for Valeria to read and he tells her secretly from time to time how to progress with Valeria's education. Gallus is interested in this. He likes educated women and he does not see why just being a girl should deprive Valeria of all the delights of learning.

Marcus has forbidden Neocles and Gallus to teach Valeria. He has very different ideas for her. He is fond of her and would not like to arrange a convenient marriage for her without her leave. Instead he hopes that she will attract a rich patrician gentleman by her modesty and beauty, and then not repel him by her learning. Marcus has heard the aristocracy talking about the unattractiveness of education in women, how they dislike the way that some women talk about politics and history and even about military strategy. It makes both them and their husbands look ridiculous, they say. Women should stay with their embroidery and their household chores. If they want something more, let them practise songs with the lyre to amuse and charm their husbands in the evening. As for those women who hunt and shoot and carouse like men, they are a disgrace to their sex.

It seems clear to Marcus that if one of his children is to marry into the patrician class, he had better concentrate on Valeria. Aemilia's children are not as elegant in their speech and manners. When he gives a banquet he always has Valeria there, looking demure and hardly speaking a word. What Marcus doesn't know is that Valeria is quiet because if she were to speak she would almost certainly betray the fact that she knows Greek and philosophy. She is fond of Marcus too,

and does not want to upset him, but she can't resist the fascinating things that Gallus has presented to her through Tullia.

In fact Marcus is worrying unnecessarily. Gallus has already fallen in love with Flavius' daughter Cornelia and plans to apply for her hand before he goes into the army in two years' time. This will connect Marcus with some of the oldest families in the Empire. He will be pleased, as Gallus knows well, and will be sure to help in every way he can. Flavius will probably make no objection, since Marcus is so rich. Gallus is a handsome boy and after all his mother's family was above reproach, so there can be no personal reason why they should not be married.

Gallus first noticed Cornelia at the little theatre of a wealthy man called Sabinus, in Alba Longa last summer. All the best people were out in the hills to escape the summer heat of Rome, and Sabinus had invited an audience to see a Greek play. Gallus noticed how attentively Cornelia listened and watched and he thought what a fitting and satisfying companion such a girl would be. It would be a terrible thing to marry a beauty and find out later that she preferred the sensational drama put on in the big theatres in Rome. And Cornelia is beautiful as well, and very lively. Gallus has seen how she enjoys the exercises at the baths. In fact it seems to him that she is a very unusual girl and that he will be fortunate indeed if he can get her.

Gallus will ask his father to arrange to have him engaged to Cornelia. He knows that she likes him, though she has no suspicion of the amount of his affection for her. Valeria is in his secret and she has been cultivating a friendship with Cornelia for the last few months. It was Valeria who told Gallus that Cornelia has begun vaguely to wonder if she will wake up one day and find herself promised to a bald old Senator. The fact that she thought of this at all makes Gallus uneasy. Perhaps without knowing it she has picked up one or two hints of a plan which her father has in mind. The betrothal will put an end to all doubts.

Gallus and Cornelia are not a bit too young to be engaged. There is a special ceremony for it, though there is no real obligation on them to get married afterwards if they change their minds, or if the fathers fall out over the money and property that belongs to the girl. By rights this should all come with her and belong to her husband after the marriage but some fathers manage to keep it in their own hands. One sure thing is that Cornelia will not have it while her husband is alive. Marcus will probably be able to arrange everything with Flavius, as they already do so much profitable business with each other.

At the ceremony, Gallus and Cornelia will promise in front of witnesses that they will be married. The witnesses will be relations from both families. Gallus will give Cornelia presents and a gold ring to wear on the wedding finger. Valeria will advise Gallus about the presents, as she knows what a girl would like. Already Gallus has spotted a jeweller in the Forum who makes beautiful necklaces and brooches. There will be a great banquet in the evening. Altogether there will be such an amount of excitement that Gallus can be fairly sure that Flavius will not try to back out of it afterwards.

He might be tempted not to let Gallus have his daughter after all if Gallus makes too much of a reputation as a poet. Especially as he specialises in satire, he could be a dangerous member of any family. The history of poets in Rome has been an uneasy one. They have a nasty knack of putting their finger on the exact spot that hurts. If they do this to the Emperor or to anyone in a high position, they may find themselves like Ovid exiled to some miserable border town where none of the inhabitants can read or write, or to a damp island, which would not be much better.

At the back of Gallus' mind is the idea that he might possibly be able to combine the advantages of the literary life

71

and the life of a businessman. He may become a Senator some day, but he can see that the whole system of government by the Senate has become cumbersome and outdated. The real governors of the Empire, apart from the Emperor himself, are the men behind the scenes, the civil servants, and the businessmen who are wealthy enough to come to the rescue of the government in time of war. These publicans, as they are called, have a bad reputation for cleaning up when the country is in difficulties, but no one can deny that they are a very useful section of the community. They are organised in joint-stock companies, with their capital held in a common fund, and they contract for all kinds of public work—provisioning ships that are going to war, collecting rents and taxes, building roads and all kinds of public buildings and importing the corn that is given out free to the people of Rome. Most of the publicans line their own pockets out of all these things, but Gallus could afford to be fairly honest.

Marcus has often tried to encourage his son to take an interest in the business side of running a great empire. He has money invested in a number of companies, and he is such a big shareholder that he has a good say in their management. The smaller shareholders are content to leave the management of the company to men of such experience.

One of Marcus' best paying investments is in a company which contracts to collect taxes in different parts of the Empire. This company has a special manager appointed by the state and changed every year, but his staff of assistants is always the same. They are expert at squeezing money out of the pockets of distant Roman citizens, who are unlikely ever to get to Rome to complain. Taxes have to be paid for the use of harbours and public pastures, and of mines of all kinds. There is a tax on wine and oil, and on all crops, and on the salt-works.

Naturally this means that Marcus is always anxious for news from the provinces. As Gallus and Neocles stroll out of the Forum, they are not surprised to see him standing under the shade of the great colonnade of the Basilica Aemilia. There is a little crowd there. Two messengers have arrived with letters. One is from Gaul, with good news of the state of the crops. There has been no war worth talking about, the rain came at the right time, and in thirty days it should be possible to begin on the harvest.

The second messenger is from a distant province in Asia, which has hardly been without a war of some sort for three centuries. The country is in a permanent state of devastation but the publicans still have to collect the taxes. They have paid good money to the state for the right to do this and now they must recoup that money, and a profit with it, from the farmers and townspeople of the province.

What are the wretched people to do? They go first to the money-lenders, of course, but after a while these demand their interest and even that can't be paid. The money-lenders haul their customers before the court and want them put in gaol, but the provincial governor points out that he can't put half the population in gaol. Who would work the land then? Next year things would be worse than ever. Better to forgive them the tax this year. Perhaps by next year they will have had time to recover.

Marcus reads the agent's letter to his fellow shareholders. They growl angrily among themselves and one or two of them make a threatening movement towards the slave who brought the letter, as if he were in some way responsible for its contents. He edges away in fright. He has trotted a thousand miles with that letter and he has not yet had time to visit his wife and children in the City. Marcus says positively:

"This can't be allowed. If the people once get the idea that they can get out of paying taxes simply by saying they can't afford it, our whole system will break down. This would be a great misfortune for the state. And think of all the small investors in our companies, who have trusted us with their

73

money—they would be ruined too. It's all the governor's fault. He should mind his own business, which is to help our agents to collect the taxes. I'll see that he gets a flea in his ear for this."

The other men seem to trust Marcus, perhaps because they know he is rather friendly with the Emperor through Flavius. They also know that the Emperor believes in the capitalist system and knows how to use the greed of the capitalists to make the Empire more powerful. He has one disadvantage in this case, and that is that he is too soft-hearted. He is quite capable of seeing the whole problem from the provincials' point of view. Usually the Pro-Consul of a province is appointed by the Senate, who draw lots for the job among themselves. The governor of this province, however, was appointed personally by the Emperor, with special instructions to reform the finances of the cities as he saw best. It will be a bad business if the Emperor backs him up in this. Marcus will try to impress on Flavius that the Emperor should at least put a stop to the crazy idea that the people should be let off paying the tax this year. He will explain that if this is done, it will be impossible to find a company willing to contract for collecting the taxes next year.

Marcus sees Neocles and Gallus standing there listening. He comes over to talk to them. He is glad to see Gallus taking an interest and he explains to him what the excitement is about. Marcus says that the present habit of getting into debt is very bad for the Empire and everyone in it. The idea that you need not pay your debts has spread from Rome to the provinces. People want to live in style and be as good as their neighbours but they don't want to wait until they have earned the money first. Some who have got themselves horribly into debt are ready to plot revolution, in the hope that things will be better for them afterwards. But the fact is, Marcus says with a calm smile, the only people who make money out of wars and revolutions are the businessmen.

At one time, he says, a very good way of making money was to go off to a war in a distant country. Egypt and Persia were very profitable. If you got in with a good general, there was lots of lovely loot to bring home. There were other possibilities as well—being made governor of a defeated kingdom, for instance. Many a young man founded a huge fortune on an opportunity like that. Lending money to a defeated king until he got his country into shape again was a good kind of business, Marcus says, though it could be dangerous. You had to be sure that the Emperor intended to restore the king to power, else you could be accused of conspiring against Rome. Then even if you saved your skin you might lose all your money, which was nearly as bad as being executed.

Nowadays things are much better. You can rely on a steady trade with the east to keep your warehouses full, and people are more inclined to buy beautiful things for their houses when they know that the times are peaceful.

While he is talking about business and money, Marcus' language becomes almost poetic. Gallus is listening at first but presently he notices that a loud argument has started at the foot of the steps. Two short, fat men are facing each other truculently. Their voices are hardened in an unmistakable way that denotes anger and attack. A little crowd is gathering. One takes a threatening step forward and says:

"Rufus is the best actor you'll ever see. No one can come near him."

"No," says the other with a sneer, "because his paunch sticks out too far."

"He is not a young man. You can't expect him to be as slim as a boy. He has dignity."

"So much that he scarcely moves at all nowadays. Perhaps he was something once but now he always reminds me of an old sheep trying to find her way out of the pen. He falls over his own feet—"

"He does not! You are so blind, you can't see him properly. Or perhaps from the back seat that you have at the theatre, you have a bad view. Your real place is at the Colosseum! You'll get action there—wham! bang! crash! That would suit you better—"

The voices are getting louder and the two main arguers are being joined by growling, gesticulating friends. At the last insult they fly at each other and in a moment the whole square seems to be full of a yelling mob, all thumping each other, tripping each other up and rolling on the ground.

Marcus, Gallus and Neocles retreat into the Basilica. When this kind of thing begins one never knows where it will end. A debtor of Marcus could take the opportunity of knifing him, for instance, in the hope that he would be able to get out of paying off his obligations afterwards. This happened to a friend of Marcus once, and when the heirs tried to prove that a certain man had done it, they found that no one would give evidence because they would not admit that they had been present at the fight.

Marcus' slaves are waiting with his litter at a side door. They get him quickly in, close the curtains and hurry home by back streets. One fight can lead to another. Riots could break out in other parts of the City, if word gets around that something is happening in the Forum.

Gallus and Neocles begin to stroll home to lunch. Behind them, they can hear the roars of the mob dying away. Neocles says:

"Such stupid behaviour! If they carry on like that, their precious old Rufus will find himself exiled in no time."

"And no loss," says Gallus. "Octavius told me he has become impossible. He expects all the other actors to come out and bow when he arrives at the theatre, and when he eats he throws the first three dishes over his shoulder to show his contempt for them."

"He would do well to throw the fourth and fifth after

them, from what I hear," Neocles says. "It's true that he's getting fat. That might be all right for a comedian but for tragedy it's ridiculous."

"It doesn't matter much either way," Gallus says. "No one could take Rufus seriously."

But thousands of Romans do take him seriously. They flock to see him, thousands together, in Pompey's theatre. The plays that they see are so melodramatic that they should not be called tragedy, but that is their traditional name. The people know the stories by heart, and they constantly interrupt with applause or groans, or with bloodthirsty yells at the nastier bits.

If the story of the play concerns a bandit, he is captured in the end and killed right there on the stage in front of all the people. A criminal who has been condemned to death is put in place of the actor for this purpose. The audience loves this and finds it very exciting, much as unthinking people nowadays get a nasty thrill out of watching violent films. There is more excuse for the Romans, however, as they have been hardened by watching the gladiators in the Amphitheatre.

As they walk home, Gallus and Neocles are surrounded by a din which would deafen anyone but a Roman. To begin with, no one speaks in a normal tone of voice. Everyone shouts harshly, to be heard above the other shouters, and the sound increases hour by hour until you would think they would lose their voices. It's a cheerful but exhausting noise, as if the people find life very exciting and want to make the most of every moment.

The streets are narrow and winding. They walk up the hill through Serpent Street, behind the great new market. Here people have placed stalls with dried and fresh beans, or tiny pieces of pickled pork or other little snacks, to tempt the customers on their way to the market. Later in the year they will have slices of melon and boiled melon seeds, and later still it will be roasted chestnuts.

78

Most sensible pedestrians keep well in off the street, lest they be trampled on by a horse or knocked down by a swaggering soldier. It is a slow progress and there are plenty of diversions. Every nation in the Empire is represented, as the foreign merchants bring samples of their goods to the market. The Italians especially enjoy the hangers-on of these foreigners, who have accompanied them to Rome and are making a few sesterces by doing conjuring tricks or showing strange animals in cages, or by snake charming. The snake charmers are Indians. They make the snakes rise up on their tails to the sound of soft, wandering, exotic music played on wooden flageolets. The passers-by are as interested in the men as they are in the snakes, they look so strange and solemn.

If the day were to turn wet, Gallus would hire a mule from the stand outside the Forum, much as you would hire a taxi nowadays. The muleteers are mostly Negro freedmen and they lead the mules for their customers. It is an uncomfortable way to travel but Gallus does not mind. If Valeria were with him, he would hire a sort of open sedan chair for her, or else send Neocles running home for a litter. Today it is quite clear and sunny, however, so that most people are on foot.

A huge litter with alabaster panels sways along, carried by eight Syrian slaves. A voice from inside calls out:

"Hello, Gallus! Head in the clouds, as usual!"

Gallus is mystified, until a cackling laugh from inside the litter tells him that it is Fabatus, a partner of his father's, who thinks that Gallus' interest in poetry is a great joke. At every banquet, when the entertainers come on he shouts to Marcus:

"Can't we have a poem from Gallus? Something about the moon rising over the Tiber to help our dinner down? Or something about a beauty he saw at the Baths?'

This is always good for a laugh from all the guests, but Gallus has had his revenge. Lately he composed a set of verses on the subject of Fabatus' habit of cruising around the Forum in his litter, on the lookout for someone to ask him to dinner. He begins by hailing a friend or acquaintance heartily, in the hope that an invitation will come spontaneously. If it does not, he moves on to another friend, to whom he confides that he has a most interesting and scandalous secret that he can't tell in the open. If this friend does not invite him to dine, he goes on to another and says that he has some good business tips but is uncertain whether or not to pass them on. Marcus has been unable to resist this one, on several occasions, though he always suspects it is a fake. But Marcus is cleverer than Fabatus and can often worm a real tip out of him, in spite of him.

As a last resort, according to Gallus' poem, Fabatus will approach a friend in the midst of a group and call out in a strong voice:

"Good morning, Senator! I was looking out for you to ask whether you said I am to dine with you tonight or tomorrow!"

Thus cornered, the Senator quickly names one or other night and Fabatus waves his porters on, delighted with himself. Gallus does not know whether these verses have reached Fabatus' ears yet. If they have not, it will certainly not be long before they do.

Lunch is an informal meal at Marcus' house, as it is at Flavius', but Marcus is less well able to resist sampling all the things that are laid out. Valeria, Aemilia and the two younger children are there, and Marcus plays with them in the garden for a while, by the fountain. They are fond of him because he is never harsh or rough with them, and almost every day he brings them little presents from the Forum. In fact they are in a fair way to being spoiled. The boy, Domitius, who is now ten years old, is his special pet. Marcus has sent all over the Empire for strange birds and dogs and other little animals for him, especially for miniature horses. He has had little carriages made for these so that Domitius can drive all around the gardens in them. The horses are lively, shaggy little things from the north of Britain. They trot with all their might, but Gallus can easily keep up with them at a fast walking-pace.

Luckily Domitius is a cheerful, healthy boy with a hearty sense of humour like his mother. Otherwise he would certainly be made into a selfish brat by Marcus. Gallus has doubts of how he will turn out, however. He is much more interested in games than in books and he can never understand why Gallus does not go to see the gladiators in the Amphitheatre. He is longing for the day when he can go himself, and he is always trying to make his little sister, Servilia, fence with him. She prefers her dolls, however, so he has to wait until he goes to the baths and meets other little boys with his own tastes. Some of these have been to the Amphitheatre with their parents. Domitius has been once only, but he was too small to see properly.

Gallus has tried to explain to him that there is no fun in watching men kill each other but Domitius says:

"It sounds very exciting. And after all they are only slaves so it doesn't matter how many we kill. The Emperor will always bring more."

Soon everyone begins to feel drowsy. It is quiet in the garden and Gallus would like to stay there listening to the fountains and watching the birds. But his eyes will not stay open. Valeria has already gone away with Tullia to lie down, in the cool of her room. Only Marcus is lively. He never wants to rest but he has been told by his doctor that it is a healthy practice to lie down for an hour in the hottest part of the day. He is beginning to think of tonight's banquet. After half an hour he springs up again and goes down to talk to Probus, the slave in charge of the dining-room.

Probus is an Egyptian who has worked in Marcus' house all his life. Marcus trusts him completely. As soon as he appears, Probus sends the other dining-room slaves scurrying out of the room. They have already begun to decorate the dining-room with flowers and plants in pots, and to hang cages of singing-birds here and there on the walls. Marcus wants to talk to Probus about the dinner that he will give to the various guests.

"There will be three different kinds of wine, like the last time," he begins, and Probus says:

"Yes, sir, like the last time."

He does not move a muscle and Marcus has no idea of what he is thinking. At the last banquet, Pliny was the guest of honour. Marcus was full of excitement when he heard that Pliny had accepted his invitation. He had refused several times. Marcus is very anxious to make friends with Pliny. He is the greatest barrister in Rome, they say, and he will talk all day, if necessary, to defend a client. Marcus never knows when he might need a friend like that.

At last he had to ask Flavius to persuade Pliny to come. This was not so easy, though it is easy enough for Marcus to squeeze Flavius. He has only to hint that he will be anxious to be paid back the money that he lent for Flavius' latest investment in Dacia. This is the Emperor's newest conquest, and Flavius borrowed a lot of money from Marcus to invest in a tax-collecting company. If he can keep his holdings, money will roll in plentifully next year. Flavius does not expect that Marcus would really make him pay back his loan now, but you can never be too careful, he thinks. He hated the job of persuading Pliny to dine with Marcus. Pliny said:

"That vulgarian? What could I possibly have to say to him?"

"He is a powerful man," Flavius said. "We must all concede something to these pillars of the Empire."

And he gave Pliny a long look which could have meant anything. Perhaps Pliny has some idea that Marcus will be useful to him some day. Whatever the reason, he sent a slave around to Marcus' house the next morning to say that he would come to dine.

At the banquet, however, he could not refrain from

commenting on the way things were done. Marcus wanted specially to honour Pliny, who is held in genuine respect by the Emperor. He does not know, though Flavius or even Probus could have told him, that Pliny is a man of modest tastes, who hates ostentation and snobbery of all kinds. Poor Marcus spent a fortune on silly things like letting down from the ceiling bouquets of flowers containing a bottle of expensive scent for each guest, and having the slaves who served the meal dressed up as Apollo and Hermes and other Greek mythical figures that no one believes in nowadays. Pliny suffered all this in silence. He even pretended to admire some of the more violent pieces of bad taste, as when a slave dressed as a gladiator rushed forward and stabbed the roast with a sword.

Pliny just raised his eyebrows when a special flagon of wine was put in front of himself and Marcus. Anyone could see that there were two other kinds, one which was served to the other guests and the last which was given to Marcus' and Pliny's freedmen.

Pliny was seated at Marcus' right, of course, in the most honourable place. The man at his other side asked:

"What do you think of our host's methods? Do you approve of them?"

Marcus heard nothing because he was leaning across Aemilia to talk to the guest on her left. Probus was pouring wine for Pliny at that moment and he heard what followed. Pliny said quietly:

"Not at all."

"What do you do yourself?" the other asked.

"I give everyone the same," said Pliny. "I've invited them to have dinner with me, not to criticise me, and if I ask them to my table I'm obliged to treat them as my equals."

"Even freedmen?"

"Yes. If they come to dinner with me, they are my companions, not just freedmen," said Pliny.

"That must cost you a packet," said the other.

"Very little, in fact."

"How can you say that?"

"Because my freedmen don't drink the same wine that I do—but I drink the same as my freedmen do."

And Pliny went on to discourse on gluttony, and how much more economical entertaining would be if the host's own tastes were simple. Marcus heard this last part, given off in Pliny's beautiful, neat Latin, and he made everyone be quiet and listen. Pliny stopped talking and smiled, and raised his eyebrows again, in a way that made Marcus want to kick him. Luckily Gallus saw that something nasty was happening and he came forward to talk to Pliny. Gallus is a kindly boy and in no time he had Pliny absorbed in a discourse on Greek poetry. Marcus began to relax. There was some point in having a son with highbrow tastes, after all.

The banquet tonight will be cosier, however. The guests will be mostly Marcus' business associates. They understand each other, and no one is put out at anything the others do on an evening out. Marcus always has a few good ideas as the night goes on, the sort of things one would not care to do if Pliny or his friend Tacitus the historian were watching. There will be a fine dinner with lots of different dishes for these rich friends but the inevitable poor clients who must be invited will be glad to get something better than hard bread and beans, which is what they would have at home. Marcus thinks there is no point in giving them bad habits. A taste of luxurious food might make them discontented with their own humble diet ever after.

When he has finished giving instructions to Probus, Marcus goes charging around the house waking everyone up to go to the baths. Gallus wants to go to the Aventine baths because they are airy and spacious, and he would have a chance of meeting Cornelia, but for the last few months Marcus has insisted on going to the newer baths by the Forum. During the spring these baths were pleasantly warm and sheltered but now that the summer has really started, the air there is damp and hot. Marcus likes the Forum better because he is more likely to meet his business friends there. As his mind is never off business for more than a few minutes together, this is a very important consideration. However, he lets himself be persuaded by Gallus, and agrees that his friends may decide for the cooler place today also. He turns out to be right in this.

Gallus enjoys listening to his father's friends talk, especially if they are Senators. Marcus is always hoping to pick up a hint of any change in government policy, which might affect his business interests abroad, but Gallus likes to hear these things for a different reason. Very soon, when he goes into the army, he is going to be caught up in the complicated system of the Empire. At first he will only be a very small part of it. This will give him time to find out how it all works, and time to discover whether or not he wants to take part in it. He has noticed that Pliny has had many government jobs, all of them responsible ones, and still he has managed to produce a large body of literary work both in poetry and in prose. Gallus and his friends admire Pliny greatly and they don't think any the less of him for having been helped on by a few highly-placed friends. Anyone wishing to be involved in running the Empire must first recognise that friends in high places are an absolute necessity, especially since the Emperor has so much personal power.

For instance, the first step a young man must take is to get himself appointed Quaestor. This is a very important office, including looking after the city's finances under the direction of one of the Consuls. To be Quaestor you have to be twenty-seven years of age. The Emperor Domitian gave that job to Pliny. Domitian was a fearsome person, who terrified the whole of Rome, yet Pliny managed never to fall out with him. Domitian was assassinated at last, when no one could stand him any more, but in the meantime he had made Pliny a magistrate. This was a suitable job for a lawyer but Pliny would have had to wait a long time for it if the Emperor had not named him. He made him prefect of the military treasury after that—the army paymaster general—and the next two Emperors kept on giving him similar jobs. Nerva, who came after Domitian, made him prefect of the treasury of Saturn, which is the place where all the City's money is kept.

Nerva was a quiet man and almost everyone enjoyed easy sleep until he died. Then came Trajan, and of course Pliny turned out to be a friend of his too. In no time at all Trajan made him Consul and then an Augur. Before the Empire, Consuls had to be elected but now it is an appointment by the Emperor himself. Since he likes to keep the reins in his own hands, there is far less work going with this job than formerly. There is no work at all involved in being an Augur, except attending an occasional meeting and being present at the readings of the symbols.

A few years later, however, Pliny got another job which did involve real work. He was made curator of the bed and banks of the Tiber and of the City sewers. The Romans are proud of their sewers, which are acknowledged to be the finest in the world. Pliny is still in charge of them and he has a large staff under his control. An Emperor once went in a boat through the sewers but Gallus cannot imagine the fastidious Pliny doing this. To keep the sewers clean there is a gang of slaves, most of whom are condemned criminals. This is an old tradition and a convenient way of making use of the criminals. They are probably rather glad to be sent to the sewers, rather than to the wild beasts for an afternoon's amusement for the people, but in fact no one thinks or cares about how they feel.

Now there is a rumour that the Emperor has still greater plans for Pliny. He has proved so honest and efficient in all his dealings with public money that he would be a very suitable person to send off as Pro-Consul to Bithynia. No one seems to be able to put the affairs of that province in order. A Pro-Consul has been there for years, a special envoy sent by the Emperor to govern the province, but he is in Rome on a visit now with a long tale of woe about the impossibility of doing anything with such a wild place. Marcus' dining-room slave, Probus, has a friend who is a slave at Flavius' house, and he says that the Pro-Consul has been visiting Flavius looking for advice. He is a lawyer but not a very good one, and he is not able to work out all the little details that have to be decided every day. When Pompey won the war against King Mithridates and got possession of Bithynia, he gave it a constitution, as the Romans do for all their new provinces. Ten Senators came out from Rome to help in this work, and to make laws for local government. Then a provincial Senate and judiciary system were set up. To a fine mind like Pliny's, details of administration present no problem, but the present Pro-Consul has tied himself in knots with them. As for developing the country, making canals, draining marshes, building bridges or anything like that, the poor man is too frantic even to consider them. For all his love of poetry and philosophy, Pliny has quite a practical and imaginative turn of mind when it comes to this kind of thing. Though he would be a great loss to Rome, he would be a benefit to the Empire in general if he were to go to Bithynia.

Gallus feels a tingle of excitement at the notion of travelling to these strange countries and seeing the wonders of other civilisations. It is a great thing to be a citizen of Rome but one of its inconveniences is that it is hard to get leave to travel. Senators and other important citizens and their sons have been limited by various old laws for hundreds of years, and may only travel in the government service. A fear that Rome will lose its population is the reason for this. It seems that the City will never forget how difficult it was to get people to stay in such an unhealthy place, at the time of its foundation by

Romulus. The laws get repealed or fall into abeyance from time to time but it is dangerous to assume that you may do as you please. If it suited someone to get rid of you, they could invoke a law dating back to Augustus or Julius Caesar and have you banished for life.

Anyone wanting to see the world would do well to be made a Consul first and then get sent to some distant country. This would mean a long wait, since you have to be forty-three years old before becoming a Consul. The advantage would be that you could be sure of being properly protected by the army and therefore safe from the bandits that roam the roads outside the cities, even in Italy. Some of these bandits are real professionals. They don't merely want the traveller's property but himself as well. They have built barracks where they take their captives and imprison them. If the man is wealthy, his family will ransom him to get him back, but if no ransom is forthcoming, then he is sold as a slave. Either way the bandit makes a fine profit.

In fact Gallus will see enough of the world when he joins the army. There is no knowing where he will be sent but it is sure to be wherever the excitement is. Gaul and Germany are quiet at the moment. Britain is said to be very damp and the inhabitants uncivilised beyond belief, so he has no wish to go there. Pontus would be interesting, though the sand-flies are man-eaters, the old soldiers say. Egypt would be the best but Marcus would have to use all his pull to get Gallus sent there. Everyone coming back from Egypt speaks well of it. Some have even adopted the Egyptian religion—worship of Isis the goddess of the Nile and patroness of medicine, marriage and agriculture. Spain would be interesting enough too, though it is said to be very like Italy. Lusitania, to the west of Spain, would be as bad as Britain. There are rumours of a wonderful green island west of Britain, with a soft, warm climate and with a great variety of birds and animals that are almost tame. They say that the seas around this island are wild and rough, making landfall difficult, but that anyone who is fortunate enough to reach it never wants to leave it again.

At the baths, where Gallus meets his friends again, these things are talked about at length. When they have been through all the ritual of the baths, they go to the library to see if any new books have come in. While the library slave is taking down a book for him, Gallus turns his head for a moment and sees Cornelia at the door, looking at him. She disappears in a moment but Gallus stands there as if he had seen a flash of lightning. She is so perfect, so calm, so beautiful, so completely Roman that he can hardly believe she could really be his. What if someone else were to get her first? He would never find another like her. He wants to run out at once and find his father, and get him to seize hold of Flavius this moment, now, before he can leave the baths, and demand Cornelia for Gallus. He takes a step towards the door and stops. It would be no use. Marcus is impossible on the day of a banquet. He can think of nothing else. But tomorrow he will be feeling a bit low and then he always praises family life and especially the virtues of the Roman matron who is able to keep her husband from excesses which are bad for his health. Tomorrow, if Gallus catches him in time, surely he can be persuaded to ask Flavius for Cornelia.

How will he live until tomorrow? Gallus does not know. Evening is coming on and everyone is beginning to go home. No one in his senses would be on the streets after dark, at the mercy of robbers and murderers of every sort. At night Rome is like a jungle, where a sudden silence is more terrifying than sound. People going to dinner with friends are accompanied by a small army of slaves. To walk alone is to invite death. Even in the daytime, if there is a big festival and everyone who can possibly manage it is at the Amphitheatre or at the Campus Martius, those who must stay at home are in danger in the quiet afternoon. The Emperor has arranged for the police to patrol in greater numbers then.

At home, Marcus runs to the dining-room at once to make sure that everything is ready. In the doorway he stops, dazzled and delighted at what Probus has been doing in his absence. He has built tall pillars of roses in a semi-circle and placed silver tables against them, decorated with peacocks' feathers. The evening sun makes the colours flash and glow. The peacock feathers are arranged in circles on the tables with the wide part trailing just over the edge. Probus says:

"As it's roast peacock tonight, I thought we would place the dishes among the feathers, my Lord."

"Perfect, perfect," says Marcus and Probus goes on without changing his expression:

"And there are cages of larks among the roses, my Lord, as it's larks' tongues for hors d'oeuvre."

"Do you think they'll sing?" Marcus asks anxiously.

"Nothing will make them sing at night, my Lord," Probus says, "but the choir of little boys will sing high, twittering notes to represent them. And I have that Egyptian dancer to go with the peacocks, the one you saw at Bassus' place last month."

"Was she expensive?"

"I'm afraid so, my Lord."

"Well, never mind. She's worth it. She'll wear peacocks' feathers, I take it?"

"Of course. She knows her business."

"Excellent, excellent. And for the lesser guests?"

"Stuffed pigs' feet and lentils, my Lord."

"Perfect. They will enjoy that. And they may see the decorations with the rest. As usual, Probus, you have thought of everything."

"The peacocks' feathers were expensive too, my Lord."

"Well, well, it can't be helped. We can talk about that to-morrow. If everyone enjoys the party tonight there will be thirty gold pieces for you and the cook and five for everyone else."

"Thank you, my Lord."

Marcus goes off to dress and Probus nips up to the loft where he sleeps, to add the thirty gold pieces on to the sum of tonight's profits. The Egyptian dancer, the peacock feathers, the boys' choir, the roses, even the larks in their cages, are none of them quite as expensive as they will appear on Marcus' bill. Probus is saving up for the day when he can have a shop beside his brother's in the Forum. Some day Marcus will give him his freedom and he will need the money to start off with.

He has a good connection among Marcus' friends, almost all of whom like vulgar and ostentatious decoration, and that is exactly what Probus' shop will supply. All during the banquet tonight, sober as a judge, he will watch the antics of the overgrown boys that are Marcus' fat, middle-aged friends, and he will dream of the day when he will be free to go to bed at sundown, and when all his work will be for his own benefit.

During the banquet, Probus watches Gallus and Valeria, and can't help wondering how they can be so dutiful and polite. The younger children are there too but they fall asleep after a while and their slaves take them to bed. When the party gets too noisy, Gallus takes Valeria's hand and hurries her away. The guests yell obscenities after them but no one has the energy to follow them. Probus has a mouthful of peacock when no one is looking. He dare not drink wine, as he has to stay awake all night. Towards morning he will be like a sheep-dog, herding wandering guests back into the dining-room when they stray around the house. That is life, he thinks, as it always was and always will be in Rome.

CHAPTER THREE

A Farmer's Family

Long before Lucius or Gallus has rolled out of bed, Tullius has been out and about his father's farm near Tibur. At the first light of day, when the owl gave her last whistle from the tall tree by the house, the whole family assembled in the atrium to offer prayers to the gods for a good day's work. Tullius' father, Decius, owns about two hundred acres of land in the fertile, hilly country twenty miles or so east of Rome. Like his brother, Flavius the Senator, he believes that Romans must always remember their origins, that their great Empire was built up by farmers and shepherds, and he says that no matter how rich a farmer becomes, he should always live on his own estate. Many of his neighbours are too lazy to do this, and have let their land to tenant farmers who don't care enough about it to keep it in good condition.

Tullius intends to follow his father's example, and has no desire to live in the noisy City. He likes a trip there now and then, to stay with his Uncle Flavius, who takes him to the Forum to listen to the orators giving off their long, well-balanced sentences. But after a while Tullius can't help thinking how like the animals they are—some braying, some neighing, some lowing, some barking—and he has to move off quietly before someone notices that he is chuckling to himself. The Roman orators take themselves very seriously.

He loves to come back to the country again, to ride slowly up the long hill to the house between the lines of still cypresses, with the fields of olives dropping away at either side. Down among them the shepherds are grazing their sheep. Decius keeps a special breed of Greek sheep that give soft, fine wool, so fine that it's worth while having two shepherds instead of one for each flock of two hundred. The shepherds are slaves and don't cost much to keep, and they live quite a long time because Decius treats them well.

Keeping these sheep out in the open is an experiment: most owners would keep them inside all the time, believing that their wool is better then, but Decius likes to try out as many new ways as he can, so that he can record them in his book of the farm. This book, he says, will be read in a thousand years' time, and will be a guide to all future Romans on how to keep the Empire in a flourishing condition. He has written some poetry about sheep, how they supply all the needs of man—cheese, wool, meat, clothing, gentle labour and an outdoor life. Tullius teased him about it, saying that Rome was founded on wolves rather than sheep, and that Decius has the best of both worlds, since he can afford to sit in his study and write poetry while his shepherds are out in the cold with the sheep.

In fact Decius works very hard, and always supervises the work on the farm himself. He has a manager but he says that things only go well if the master himself is always on the spot. The manager's name is Regulus. He is a slave, but an intelligent one, and he hopes to have a farm of his own some day when he is freed. For this reason he watches Decius' methods very carefully, so as to be able to use his knowledge when his own time comes. His farm will not be anything like as big as Decius', but it will be near Rome too, so that he can sell fancy produce to the rich people in the City.

Decius' system is to have some of everything, including the silly luxury things that the Romans like to eat at banquets.

He sells direct to the houses of the Senators whom he knows through his brother, keeping in touch with the slaves and freedmen who organise the dining-rooms. Probus always buys from Decius when there is a banquet at Marcus' house, and that is sometimes several times a week.

Decius finds it worth while to keep a small flock of peacocks and an aviary full of small birds which are all called larks or quails. Most of them actually are larks and quails but in general any small bird, once it's plucked and cleaned, can be given a leg-up into a more aristocratic category. Regulus often slips in a few sparrows when Decius is not looking. He keeps dormice fattening in jars too, and often gets an order for a few dozen of them.

He doesn't care for fancy food, though he has tasted everything he produces himself, on principle. He keeps pigeons and chickens and ducks, which he regards as more reasonable in every way, and they have the advantage of keeping the slaves busy in any spare moments between heavier jobs. The whole economy of farming depends on using every moment profitably. He keeps his sheep only two years before killing them and selling the meat and the skins. This kind of thinking is what makes him so successful.

Decius' house is fine and spacious, set in a compound, with an open central atrium which is cool in summer and gives shelter from the wind in winter. It's a short winter, only seven or eight weeks, but sometimes a cold wind from the mountains can be quite unpleasant. There is no central heating through the hot-water pipes, though there is a system that heats the water for the baths and for the kitchen. A special slave keeps the furnace supplied with wood and stokes the fire when it's needed.

A rather unpleasant smell hangs about the atrium at all times because just beyond it are the pigs and poultry, where they will be safe from thieves, animal and human. At present Decius keeps only a few pigs, in a small shed adjoining the house, but he has plans for going into them in a big way.

The living-rooms open off the atrium at one end of the compound. There is a dining-room, a drawing-room and four bedrooms for the family. Beside them is the bakery and then the kitchen, a small room with no window. The only light comes from the door that opens into the atrium. The smell in the kitchen is truly terrible, between the smoke from the fire in the middle of the room and the manure in the adjoining stable. The door between is always being opened and shut as the slaves go in and out with food and bedding for the animals. Tullius has suggested more than once that the animals could be housed a few yards away but his parents won't hear of it: farm smells are healthy, they say, and people can become accustomed to them in time. The two slaves' dormitories are above the kitchen and partly over the stables. Naturally, they never complain.

At the other end of the compound, all the oil- and wine-making goes on in a number of special rooms. On this June day, the grapes are hard and green on the vines and the olives are so small that they can scarcely be seen against the leaves. Harvesting them will come in the autumn but making the wine is a slow process and takes most of September and October. Everything has to be done exactly, so as to keep the most perfect flavour, because Decius' wine has a good reputation. Pliny recommends it to his friends as an honest wine that one need never be ashamed of, though it's not too expensive for everyday use. Pliny always poses as a plain, ascetic man but though his tastes are simple they are exquisite. No use trying to palm off a thrush for a quail on him. He has visited Decius' farm many times and has said that he has learned more honesty in an hour there than he learned in five years from his colleagues in the Senate. He puts things so strongly that his words are often repeated, and Decius found that suddenly he had more customers than he could supply. Tullius said privately that he had never seen so many fox-faced men in his life as came to buy wine from the honest man, but after a while they moved on to someone else, probably hoping for a better bargain.

The wine-press has a very long room to itself. It is a complicated piece of machinery made of wood, consisting of a beam forty feet long which can be raised and lowered by means of a windlass, pressing the juice out of the grapes and sending it flowing down an earthenware tunnel into vats where it can ferment. There is an oil-press too, but making olive oil is a fairly easy task by comparison with the vintage.

When the time comes to pick the grapes, Decius always begins the day with special prayers to the gods, for fine weather and a well-flavoured wine which he will later offer in sacrifice. Before the first pickers arrive he is out in the vineyard, overseeing the knives to make sure that they are sharp enough. A blunt knife would tear the main branch of the vine and damage it. Forty pickers are employed to cut the bunches of grapes carefully and place them in baskets, which are then emptied into carts drawn by the big, slow, white oxen. These are brought home and the grapes are piled into the press, the slaves lower the beam and the juice comes trickling out. Decius always tastes the first drops to see if they are up to their usual standard, then catches a small bottle of the juice to offer to the gods in the evening. The vineyard is on a sunny hill, with just the right amount of drainage, and this ensures that the flavour is always excellent. Still, everyone in the household waits excitedly until he smacks his lips and says:

"Good! At least as good as last year!"

Regulus knows that he will get twenty gold pieces when all the wine is made but this is not the only thing that keeps him at work. He loves the vintage, and as he is younger than Decius he can run from one part of the press-room to another, and out to the room where the fermentation vats are, so fast that the other slaves say he is in ten places at once.

97

Everyone works well, and the slaves down among the grapes laugh and joke among themselves and tell stories about their owners.

They don't all belong to Decius: he hires twenty-five of them from a contractor and pays a lump sum for their work, as well as providing bread for their lunch in the hottest part of the day. They must have a rest then too, according to the terms of the agreement, as their owner has promised them for other work later in the season and he wants to make sure they stay alive for that. In August they come to Decius' farm for the threshing and they pick the olives in early December too.

The fermentation vats are sunk up to their necks in the earth floor to keep them cool. The room is at the far end of the compound, away from the kitchen and the furnace room, and there are a great many apertures in the walls to allow the air to circulate. In a few weeks, when the juice is fermented, it is ladled off into jars and put into the wine-store to mature for a few months. Some people drink their wine almost at once but Decius gives his at least a year before he gets a jar down to try it. Only when he has tasted it himself does he begin to sell it off to his customers.

Decius' most profitable crop is grapes, dessert grapes for the City market and to be made into raisins, and also grapes for wine. Each has to be treated differently. The first of the dessert grapes will go straight to the market, to be sold juicy and fresh. Roman grapes are fat and firm and light-coloured, and keep very well for a few weeks. After a while, however, they get wrinkled and soft, if they are not put in pots with covers and buried in the refuse from the wine-press, or kept in grape-juice or in wine. Though this blackens the stems it is possible to keep the grapes until February or March when people will pay a fine price for them. Some grapes which will be made into raisins are spread on flat stones to dry in the sun, or hung up in the blacksmith's workshop where the heat of the fire will dry them out.

Decius grows melons in a big way too—in the middle of April he had the side of a huge, south-facing hill planted with them, to be ripe in August. A line of slaves went out with baskets of seeds slung on their backs and planted them one by one, beginning at the top of the field and never stopping until the whole hill was covered. When the melons are harvested, they will be taken to Rome and sold to dealers who will set them in great piles by the City gates and stay with them until they are all sold. Decius also has big fields of wheat but he has decided to reduce his planting of it, since so much wheat comes more cheaply from distant parts of the Empire.

Up where the wine is kept, there are other rooms for storing dried figs and raisins. Some green grapes are kept there too, sprinkled with dry bran to take up any damp that may get in. There is a special space for cheeses, and jars of pickled vegetables, and pomegranates, whose tough skins make them good for keeping. In shelves on the walls, dried herbs for cooking are spread out, making the air of the whole room smell deliciously.

Tullius' mother, Lavinia, and his sister, Clodia, look after the store-room themselves, though they have a housekeeper to see to the cooking and keep the kitchen slaves in order. Neither Lavinia nor Clodia would care to spend much time in that dirty, smoky hole, but they feel that it's quite good enough for the slaves. Lavinia knows from conversation with her friends that good treatment spoils slaves for work, and it's unpleasant to have to hang the worst of them in order to teach the others a lesson. Decius hardly ever does this—he says that a good beating is just as effective and you have your slave for work afterwards as well.

Lavinia's and Clodia's special care is for the wool. There is a bench under the verandah in the shade, where they can have a huge basket of wool brought in, already washed, and they sit there by the hour and card it into soft rolls ready for spinning. Clodia loves this work. She is fourteen, two years younger than Tullius, and though she likes the life on the estate she always wants to hear stories about the great world outside. Wool-carding time is always the best for this. They have no sooner settled down to work than one of the house slaves, who is helping, says:

"What story shall we have today?"

Lavinia pauses for a moment to think and then she says:

"Let's begin with the story of the wife who turned into a dragon on her wedding-night."

"A dragon! On her wedding-night!"

"It happened in Thrace, a long way from here," Lavinia begins comfortably, and then she's off on the story.

Clodia knows that she makes up these stories as she goes along, but the slaves listen with shrieks of terror, as if they were hearing about something that actually happened. In a little while, Clodia herself begins to believe the story too, her mother tells it so well, pausing now and then to make sure that everyone is leaning forward tensely, gathering in all the eyes with her own and holding them steadily, lowering her voice almost to a whisper before telling the worst, the very worst thing that happened, while all the time her hands never stop moving with her carders, rolling the wool, tossing the roll into the basket, picking up a new piece, rolling that, and so on throughout the long afternoon.

When Tullius' tutor, Eumenes, tells the stories, they are not quite so exciting but Clodia finds that she always remembers them ever after. Eumenes is a Greek slave and his stories are all true ones of the Greek heroes. Though he doesn't say so, it's clear that he thinks the Greeks are superior in every way to the Romans, more disciplined, better athletes, better soldiers, better poets and playwrights. He stands quietly by a pillar while he talks and everyone listens respectfully, though he seems always to pick rather lugubrious stories with a moral to them.

Clodia has noticed that educated slaves are never quite as happy as the ordinary ones who spend all their time at farm and housework. When she asked her mother about this, Lavinia said it was quite true, that naturally the ignorant ones don't understand their position and can therefore forget about it for long periods, whereas an educated slave is always regretting the loss of his freedom and despising his masters. She says one must keep patience with them because it's not easy to get a good slave who cares enough about learning to pass it on even to his enemies.

Clodia doesn't like to be called an enemy. She likes Eumenes, though he is very critical, because he has taught her to read and write. This is more than her mother could do for her. He has also taught her to play the lyre, so that she can entertain the company when there is a party. The music she plays is very refined, not in the least like the noisy bangings that the slaves make at the feast of Saturnus, when they take over most of the house and run and shout and play all night long. Eumenes doesn't take any part in this, even though he is a slave, and what he has taught Clodia above all is that self-respect is the most lasting of all the virtues.

Decius is not too pleased to see Clodia so attached to Eumenes' kind of learning; he says that a farmer's daughter should be made of tougher stuff. Lavinia reminds him that the best Roman women had all the virtues and learning as well, and after all Clodia is very good at domestic arts. Besides, Decius is so rich that he can afford an educated daughter. And besides, if she were ignorant she would never be invited to Uncle Flavius' house, where there is very good company, and where some rich Senator might take a fancy to her. And besides, Decius can't call himself just a farmer when he makes so much money on the Stock Exchange.

When the basket is full of rolls of soft wool, the spinning-wheels are brought out and four of them are worked together by Lavinia and Clodia and two slaves. Clodia is not yet as good as her mother at spinning—it's said that it takes seven years to make a good spinner. If she takes her eye off the thread for a second, a little fat lump appears on it, or else it gets so thin that it breaks and has to be joined with spit and worked through again. Lavinia is able to spin by the hour, a perfect, thin thread streaming from her right hand while her left hand holds the spindle as steady as a rock. A spider couldn't do better. She makes a thread so fine that Decius sometimes sells some of it to his most particular customers for making togas with, as a great compliment, though he makes them pay well for it. Fine woollen cloth is very rare in Rome, he says, and people should learn to appreciate it.

There is a loom upstairs, beside the store-room, for making woollen cloth, but this is work for a man slave, and a strong one at that, the shuttles and treadles are so heavy. Lavinia supervises the work and decides what dyes will be used if coloured cloth is needed. Most of the cloth is white, bleached by the fuller after it is woven. Human urine is one of the most useful bleaching ingredients and the fullers in the City keep special jars outside their shops into which passers-by can obligingly perform, a convenience for both parties. Decius sends his cloth into Rome to be bleached, because it would not be worth while to keep a whole fuller's workshop for his own household.

The wool of darker sheep is spun for rougher clothes, army cloaks and the heavy, hooded cloaks that the slaves wear if they work outside in the winter. Vegetable dyes are used for colours, but not much dyeing is done. Lavinia has a marvellous story about a shepherd who pleased the gods so that they rewarded him by turning his sheep all the colours of the rainbow. Thus he became rich, since everyone was eager to have his wool.

Altogether the sheep are much more important than the cattle on the farm. Decius breeds cattle for work, for pulling ploughs and wagons, and to sell to the butcher who supplies

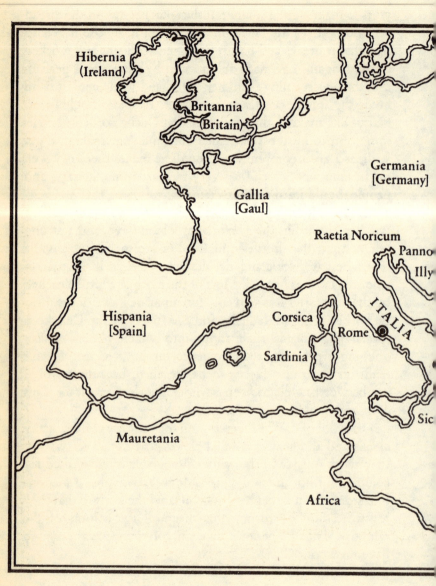

The Roman Empire in the time of Trajan

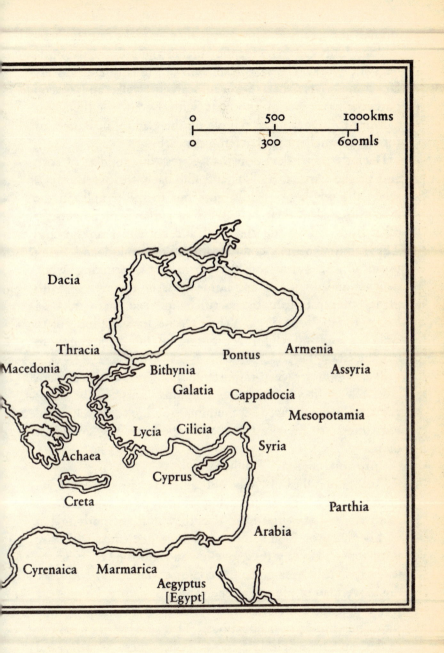

500   1000kms

300   600mls

Dacia

Thracia   Pontus   Armenia

Macedonia   Bithynia   Assyria

Galatia   Cappadocia

Mesopotamia

Lycia   Cilicia

Syria

Achaea   Cyprus

Creta   Parthia

Arabia

Cyrenaica   Marmarica

Aegyptus
[Egypt]

animals for sacrifice. This means that he picks out the best-looking bulls and cows for the butcher and sells the strongest ones for work. The sacrificial bulls are usually enormously fat, some so fat that they can scarcely walk, and several butchers have special contracts with Decius for them, for sacrifice to Jupiter in his temple on the Capitol in Rome, or for sale to smaller country temples nearby.

Decius' special devotion is to Ceres, the goddess of corn and of the harvest. Tullius and Clodia both love the days when the whole household goes out to the temple on the estate, dressed in their best, wearing garlands of flowers, to offer lambs and cattle and fruit and corn in thanksgiving. The country people come from miles around and bring bread to eat, sitting on the warm grass, drinking wine, dancing and singing, going home at last in the evening with plenty of meat from the sacrifices to keep them full and happy for the next week. When Decius took Tullius out to walk the land and tell him various useful things about how to run the estate, he said:

"Feast days are very important, so be sure to keep them always, even if you don't feel religious yourself. The slaves and the tenants need something to look forward to, something to dress up for and celebrate. It's good for them."

"Are you religious?" Tullius asked.

"Religion is the only hope of Rome," Decius said earnestly. "I'm in the business of supplying luxuries to the upper classes and I can tell you first-hand that they think of nothing but bodily pleasures, food and drink and women, and yet they're not happy. They say they love life and still they're weary of it. They hardly ever go to the country where they could see the movement of life and all the variety of nature. Pliny and a few others have the sense not to let their days slip by in a thousand tiny pre-occupations. That's why they're not restless and miserable like most of the others. Cruelty and

bloodshed and fighting will be the ruin of Rome, mark my words, if men don't see the light."

As he talked, Decius became more and more gloomy. To cheer him up Tullius asked:

"Why do you pay so much attention to Ceres? What about Jupiter and Neptune and Juno and Apollo and Mars and Venus and all the others?"

"Since Jupiter is the father of all the gods, he benefits when we pay homage to any of them," Decius said. "I never go to sea, and we live so far from the shore that I don't have to consider Neptune too much. Juno will be pleased if Jupiter is, as every wife is happy when her husband is happy. Since Apollo helps the harvest to ripen, he is indirectly honoured when we honour Ceres. Between you and me, Venus gets plenty of attention in the City and won't miss mine. As for Mars, when you go to war with the army will be time enough to attend to him. That leaves Ceres, the goddess who feeds us all with the healthiest food and always sends us a good harvest. Pin your faith on Ceres and you'll never go in want."

"What about the new god, the single god that is said to rule the whole world?"

"I've heard of him, but he seems a very dangerous one to me. According to the people who believe in him, all men are equal. If that were true, the slaves would have to be freed, and who would do the work? The rich would have to share with the poor, and there just wouldn't be enough to go round. All men are not equal, as we can see by opening our eyes. Some are clever, some are stupid, some are born rich, some poor, some are ugly, some beautiful, some healthy and some delicate. How can anyone in his senses say they are all equal?"

"The idea is to try to make them equal, to make them improve themselves so that the nations can all live happily together."

"The Roman Empire would disappear if that were ever to come about," said Decius. "And as long as the world exists, there will always be some people who don't want to live at peace with their neighbours. Men can't be improved much—not in this life, at least."

"Then you believe that man is immortal?"

"Certainly. Otherwise how should men ever see the ghosts of those who died? We know that our Generals have often been warned in sleep about the dangers of the next battle, by a long-dead General who is still watching the course of our history. These spirits have revealed that the way to heaven lies in doing our duty in this life. Some say it will be a great pleasure to be freed from the anchor of flesh and bone, and released into eternal life. We're specially fortunate, having such a good life here to begin with."

It is true that Decius loves his farm so much that he never wants to leave it and hardly seems to notice how hard he has to work. Tullius knows another side of farming, however. Now and then he rides over in the morning to visit Gaius, a man he greatly admires, an old soldier who has a small farm a few miles away, across the valley where the land is not so rich. Gaius was given the farm after one of the Emperor's campaigns and he was glad to get it because he felt too old to go to war again.

"Funny thing," he said to Tullius, "those Generals never seem to get tired. It's not just that they have chariots and horses, while most of us are on the two feet we were born with. We all eat much the same food. We wear much the same weight of clothes—indeed ours are often warmer because we don't go in for fancy stuff. Rough wool and leather is all we ever asked for. But a General—that's what we always called the Emperor—a good one, mind you—could run us off the ground. I remember the time when we were on the last campaign, out in some godforsaken corner of the Empire with nothing but wild animals and uncivilised natives to be seen, and the General got us all out on the march in the month of January, with the snow falling and the ice splitting the rocks, and ran us across a mountainside to lay siege to a city that none of us had ever heard of before.

"Halfway up the mountain, we went on strike, a dangerous enough thing, you'll say, but we didn't tell what we were doing. We just went slow, a trick that every seasoned soldier knows, and my lord was away off ahead of us with the crack troops, gone out of sight before the first day was over. But when we got over the top of the mountain, at the dawn of the next morning, what did we see? The Romans, by Jupiter, surrounded by the enemy, all brandishing their savage weapons and yelling outlandishly, galloping up and down on little black horses. That broke our hearts. We charged down that mountainside like a pack of wild bulls, and attacked from behind and scattered the whole lot of them. The enemy thought it was all a clever trick but the General knew better. We could barely look at him, we were so ashamed of having abandoned him, but all he said was: "Better late than never." He could have had us all done in there and then for treachery but that was all he said. Now I make out that a General is a different kind of man from the rest of us, the gods have a special interest in him, he's made bigger and stronger to begin with, and he can endure more heat and cold than an ordinary man. He has more patience too: he can lay a plot as well as any fox, and bide his time until the moment comes to strike.

"My grandfather used to talk about the campaign in Germany, how the Germans were terrified at the very sight of the Roman army. It seems they don't have augurs like ours, only women prophets who read the signs by watching eddies in the streams and the movement and noise of rivers. Well, these women warned the Germans that they shouldn't go to battle until the next moon, or some such nonsense— though they could see the army of Rome out there before them, I ask you! So what did they do? Squealing and squeaking with fright, they still camped down there and then and waited for the moon to change.

"Our General had word of what was happening, because he had a very good spy system, with Roman soldiers from other campaigns who had married into the enemy country, as always happens. Well, one of these spies told him what was going on and he said: 'Why wait for the moon?' It got to be a kind of saying in the army afterwards. And of course he attacked, and chased the poor devils all the way to the Rhine. Eighty thousand they killed, my grandfather said, and he wasn't given to exaggerating. The Germans that were left, and their General too, had to get across the Rhine as best they could. Good enough for them, too, after attacking Gaul for no good reason except that they wanted to grab the land."

"It seems all wars are fought for land," Tullius said.

Gaius laughed.

"You might say I fought my wars for land too, since that was all I got out of it. In the old times, I'd have been given a stake in some benighted outpost of the Empire, with orders to polish off any barbarians that would put their noses too close. I wouldn't care for that job, though even nowadays I'd have got a better spot if I had stayed in the army reserve a few years longer. You get enough of wars, and that's the truth. Funny how I didn't mind killing men long ago and now I can hardly bring myself to kill a cock for the soup. Gone soft, I suppose. I notice lots of my old buddies are the same—some of them spend their days weaving and spinning like women, glad of a quiet life, I suppose."

"Did you know something about farming before you went into the army?"

"Not a thing. But my wife Melvia did. Her father was a tenant farmer in the Campania, and her uncle here in Latium. The uncle kept only sheep but she learned from her father how to look after a mixed farm, with a bit of fruit and a few olive trees and vines. It's hard work when you can have only one or two slaves. Lazy devils they are, too, and we don't seem to have much luck with ours. They all seem to die at twenty-one or twenty-two, though my neighbour Decimus has his a few years longer."

"He has a proper shed to keep his in," Melvia interrupted. She was stirring the bean soup on the charcoal fire, tasting it every now and then and adding a pinch of this herb or that. "We haven't had a slave for two years, in any case. We can't afford to feed one. My father always kept a few but I never liked the idea of owning slaves—it didn't seem right to have something that looked so like a man but was handled like an animal. Decimus just says they're the same as the oxen, only better able to look after themselves. It's not true, though. The oxen never revolt, and the slaves have done it several times. I'll tell you what, sir: I wouldn't like to be some of those big landowners down south, that keep an army of slaves and never do a hand's turn themselves. What's to stop those slaves from turning around some day and doing in their owners? There's enough of them there to do it—hundreds and thousands. Any night they could murder everyone in their beds."

"Now, Melvia," said Gaius, "what's the use of expecting misfortune? It comes anyway, and never in the form you thought it would. Tell me, sir, how is the wheat up at your place?"

"Almost ripe. It's rather early, in fact, though we had such a lot of cloud. How is yours?"

"Fair enough. I'd say we'll be threshing early. We had good beans, well-filled and in good condition for keeping too. They look fine at this time of the year but we get sick of beans by the time winter is over, though I must say that Melvia makes a fine bean soup at all times of the year. And the vines look very healthy. Decimus has a kind of mould on his, I don't know why. Funny thing about Decimus, he has plenty of luck in some ways and in others he seems to do worse than anyone. Of course he's too stingy to pay for sacrifices to the gods at the proper seasons, so what can he expect? I've told him over and over again that the only reason I'm alive today is that my father always offered a lamb and a jug of wine before I went off to battle, not only to Mars but to Neptune as well, in case some lunatic General would take us across the sea, as they frequently did. Then he'd do the same when he heard I was coming home, not waiting until he saw me walking into the house as another would do—oh, no. He had been a soldier himself, and he said the most dangerous part was the last few miles of the road home. Of course in his day, the roads were hopping with bandits and thieves of all sorts and sizes but the times are a little better now. Do you know what I'd really like to own? I saw it in the north, near the mountains, but not right in the mountains—a lovely, quiet wood of oak trees, and a herd of pigs feeding underneath them. It looked so peaceful and harmless. I'd stay all day minding pigs."

"What about the smell?"

"You don't notice that in the open air. Pigs are the best stock of all. You can always sell them: every inch of a pig can be sold, right down to the tail."

He was silent for a while, thinking about pigs. Then he said:

"I'll be over one of these days to ask your father's advice about peacocks. They're a rather fancy kind of poultry for the like of us but I've heard good reports of them, that they don't eat too much and that they fatten early."

"But they screech before rain."

"I do that myself, with the pain in my joints," said Gaius with a laugh. "Sleeping on the ground, in a tent or out in the open, doesn't set you up in your health for life, I can tell you. I wouldn't mind their screeching, if I got a good price for them."

"When you think it over," Tullius said eagerly, "which was your most exciting campaign?"

"Campaigns, campaigns! I know what's going on in your head. I remember well how excited I used to be. I remember the smell of the horses, and how they used to neigh and paw the ground when we were within a few hours of setting off, feeling the tightness in the air, and I remember the lantern light shining on the big mule carts that had to be loaded from the night before, with food and tents and weapons. Oh, it was exciting, all right. The first time, I almost forgot to pray, as I had promised my father to do."

"Was the first one the best, then?"

"No, I can't say it was. I got so tired, for one thing, and I didn't know the ropes, didn't know a soldier should always have a hunk of bread hidden on him somewhere in case the commissariat breaks down, didn't know a soldier should never miss a chance of a pee—that sort of thing. In a way, the last campaign was the best, not that I ever enjoyed the fighting part of it but the Emperor never treated the enemy too badly when they were defeated. He always had an eye to building up the conquered country for the good of the Empire and we were instructed not to do too much laying waste. That meant the people were nice to us, the girls would bring us home and get their mother and their auntie to cook up a good feed and maybe lay on a few other comforts as well."

"Now, now, less of that!" Melvia warned him.

"Well, that's how it is in wars. We used to get lonely, far from home, and you'd give anything for a kind word. I was in the first cohort of the legion, nine hundred and sixty men, and we looked very smart in those days, though you wouldn't think it to look at me now."

"You had the Eagle, then," Tullius said in awe.

"That's right. Funny thing about the Eagle, you knew it was really nothing and still you'd give your life for it. We wouldn't let a barbarian soldier lay a hand on it, though they were as much in the army as we were. Good enough for them to have charge of the horses. But we old Roman soldiers had the honour of marching out there in front, proud as peacocks—did I tell you I was thinking of keeping a few peacocks?"

"Yes. What was the farthest part of the Empire that you were in?"

"Parthia, I suppose, a hell of a long way from here, I can tell you, if you had to walk all the way to Brindisi first. And on the way home, the last time, the storm that got up seemed to be a special job for us. I thought my last hour had come. The rowers were hardly able to make any headway against the wind and the tide, and there was no question of turning back, we were so far from the land when the storm blew up. When I got home, I can tell you that Neptune got a fat ram from me, though at that stage I had sworn that I'd never lay eyes on his lousy element again as long as I lived. But you never can be sure, and that's why I didn't take the risk. Melvia's uncle was caught out like that—thought he was living a quiet life, out on his farm under Vesuvius, growing fruit for the market, keeping a few sheep, not a care in the world, when suddenly the whole mountain blew up behind his back and burned him out of house and home. He got away alive, with his family, and I can tell you it made a religious man of him. He said they were a bad lot in Pompeii, asking for trouble, and they got it in the end, as we all will if we don't watch out."

"We couldn't rise to a ram now, for Neptune or anyone else," Melvia said. "Tell him your new idea, Gaius."

"She doesn't like it. It's not like keeping peacocks." Gaius seemed very nervous indeed but after a moment he threw back his shoulders and said: "After all, it's not so strange for a man who has been in the army. I was a centurion, with eighty men under me all the time. I got to know them pretty well, with practice. I could tell which ones would turn out well and which were the weaklings. I'm thinking of going into the slave business. There, I knew you wouldn't like it either. What's wrong with it, I'd like to know? Everyone keeps slaves, including your father. Someone must handle them, buy them, sell them, just the same as someone must buy and sell the oxen and the sheep and—and the peacocks. Where's the difference?"

"A slave is a man."

"We all know that. He's a special kind of man—we know that too. A good slave-trader is a benefit to the whole community, to the slaves too. I have a little bit put by, enough to buy five of them to begin with—"

"Five! Where would you keep them?"

"In the kitchen at first, then when I make some money out of them, we should be able to build a proper shed for them. I'd feed them properly too, and let them worship with the family every day, since we know they are men. I'd keep only clean, healthy slaves and build up a good reputation for them. Then after a while I'd breed some of my own—you can sell them after seven years or so, if they're in good condition. I'd train my own slaves on the land, give them a few skills and get better prices for them, and I'd have free labour from them as long as they lived with me. The best are the Egyptians. I know too much about the Germans—they're only good for work in the fields, though they're clever enough when they like. I'd treat them well, I tell you."

Tullius believed that he would try. Gaius was a kindly man at heart, and knew from his experience in the army what it was like to be hungry and cold. Until Eumenes came along, Tullius had scarcely thought about slaves—they were there to do the work, you loved them as you loved your dog, but you knew that when one died it was no tragedy. Eumenes changed all that, talking for minutes on end about the position of slaves in Greece, always in that quiet, soft voice, never a hint that he might be complaining about his own situation, just giving the facts.

A Greek slave is as well off as anyone else, Eumenes says, if anything better off, because he is sure of his job. A free man who has no family to care for him might go hungry for months, if the season were bad or if his village were sacked during a war. A free man himself, Eumenes was captured and carried off in this way, and sold in the market in Rome, and though he had owned slaves of his own, he had no idea of how to protect himself. Slavery is bad for the upper classes, he says, because they gradually lose their skills and especially their self-discipline. At this point Tullius feels his scalp begin to tingle, a sign that he is learning something very nasty but useful.

"We don't really believe in slavery," says Eumenes. "It's not a Greek tradition. In Greece slaves wear the same clothes as free men, they are paid regular wages, they mix freely with everyone else and move about wherever they like, not chained up or tied up as they often are here. The only difference is that they're not full citizens, though they become so as soon as they are freed."

"Slaves wear the same clothes as free men in Rome too," Tullius says, "or almost the same."

"Yes, but for the wrong reasons. If they wore different clothes the slaves themselves might wake up to the fact that there are a lot of them there, enough to stage a successful revolt. Not that they'll ever do it again, after what happened under Crassus."

Eumenes knows a lot of Roman history. He lets a long silence fall, to give Tullius time to think of that terrible time, almost two hundred years ago, when the slave Spartacus organised an army of ninety thousand fellow slaves and terrorised the whole of Italy for two years, but was defeated in the end, and he and many of his comrades were crucified at either side of the road, all the way from Capua to Rome. And in Nero the Emperor's time, only fifty years ago, the City Prefect, Lucius Pedanus Secundus, was killed by one of his own slaves whom he had ill-treated, and he and every slave in the household was executed as a penalty for the crime. Great crowds of citizens, armed with stones and torches, came out to protest against the verdict of the Senate, asking at least to have the women and children spared, but the Emperor insisted that the law be enforced. It was because of this affair that Decius would never live in Rome but swore to spend his life in peace in the country where, even though he kept slaves, he could follow Pliny's custom and treat them like friends—humble friends, but worthy of politeness and consideration.

At last Eumenes said:

"A better time will come. You may even live to see the day when a good Emperor—not that our Emperor is not the best we deserve—may set up laws to protect the slaves."

"But what can he do? They're the property of their masters."

"He could enact a law forcing the masters to sell all their slaves, if it could be proved that they are unusually cruel or that they have killed any of them. That's only one idea. An Emperor will be sure to think of plenty more."

Melvia was watching Tullius while he thought over these things and remembered the doubts that Eumenes had implanted in his mind. She said softly:

"Tell him what you think, sir. Go on, tell him it wouldn't be a right thing for him to breed slaves like animals, to ask me to throw them their mash the way you would to a calf. What's all right for the rich is all wrong for the poor. The gods will strike him for it."

"Nonsense, woman! Have the gods struck Rome? Tell her to have sense, sir. Tell her that a man has to make out a living somehow. We can't live on air."

Melvia shrieked:

"The gods haven't struck Rome yet but who's to say they won't do it tomorrow?"

"They'll strike us, if you talk like that."

"Why don't you set yourself up with pigs?" Tullius asked quickly. "You said you like pigs: they would be at least as profitable as slaves, you could keep more of them, you could eat one now and then, they've never been known to revolt. Pigs would be much better."

"You think so?"

"Yes. Pigs and peacocks would go well together. I can help you with them, as it happens, because my father has just arranged for me to have a herd of pigs of my own, to start me off on farming, he says. I think he wants to take my mind off the wars, though he knows I'll have to join the army for a while, at least. Only yesterday he was talking about giving me the son of his old swineherd, Scrofa—you remember Scrofa?"

"Yes, yes, a knowledgeable man. His son is called Hector, I think."

"Yes, they call him that for fun, because he's such a little weed, but he really has a way with pigs, my father said, and he'll have charge of them."

"How many?"

"A hundred, or perhaps a hundred and fifty. He's going to buy ten sows in Tusculum, and a boar from the north, because Scrofa is a great believer in having a good boar. I've often heard him say: 'The offspring will be more like the sire than the dam.'"

"I don't believe that," said Melvia. "And talking of pigs, did you ever hear the story of the sow that was so fat, she couldn't stand up, and a shrew-mouse ate a hole in her flesh and built a nest in it, and had a brood of young mice in there?"

"Then we could breed shrew-mice at the same time," said Gaius, glad to have her in good humour again. "What else does Scrofa say?"

120

"He likes pigs not too big, nor too fat, because he says they're healthier in every way if they're able to move about. Ten sows will have twelve piglets each, that makes one hundred and twenty, and if we keep the sows for seven years that will make eight hundred and forty, and with the ten sows and the boar that will make eight hundred and fifty-one to feed. Double that, and subtract the ten sows—"

"Wait! Wait! Would I have to be able to do sums like that before I could keep a herd of pigs?"

"It would help, but I'll do the sums for you. He said we should have two litters a year, one in July and one in January. The first lot would be weaned in time to eat the stubble grass after the harvest, and the second lot could be sold as sucking-pigs—there's a big price for them in Rome in winter, and that's the exact time when the sows won't have enough milk for them. We're to keep some of them and feed them on beans—"

"The whole country lives on beans in the winter-time."

"And we can store some mast for them, if they haven't eaten it all in the autumn. Scrofa has ideas about the kind of sty we'll need too, if we're going to go in for pigs in a big way."

"I could never afford a sty," said Gaius. "When I thought of pigs, I thought of free grazing in an oak wood, like that one I saw in the north."

"What about that bit you have put by? You'll get far more for it in pigs than you would in slaves. You'll probably be able to afford a sty as well, especially if I lend you my boar and you only have to buy some sows."

"What would the sty be like? Perhaps it wouldn't cost too much."

"Scrofa says there must be a sty for each sow, else the piglets get all mixed up. Sows don't know their own litter from the next."

"What matter if they get mixed up?"

"He says it spoils the breed. So you need a row of sties, with a four-foot-high wall between each pair so that the sow can't jump over, and a threshold low enough for the sow to get out but high enough to keep the piglets in."

"That makes sense. So if I had two sows, I'd only need two sties."

"Correct. When the piglets are born, if the litter is a big one you can sell off some quite soon and just let the sow keep eight or possibly ten, if she's able to feed them. Those can be sold at a year old, and there's always a good market for them too."

"It seemed to me that the Roman army lived on salt pork," said Gaius. "And I must say it's good grub when you're hungry, though it was often so salty that we nearly died of thirst afterwards, unless there was plenty of water about. I saw a lot of pig-farming when I was with the army. A funny thing, here we think of pigs as being slow, harmless creatures but I saw pigs when I was on the German campaign, kept by a tribe called the Belgae, and they were more like wolves for speed and wickedness. They lived out in the open —the pigs, I mean—and though it's a cold climate, they never seemed to come to any harm. I wouldn't mind getting a few sows from there, and trying out the breed. But they'd probably go soft after a while in this climate."

"The Romans like their pork and ham fat," Melvia said. "You have to give the housewife what she wants."

"That's true," said Tullius, "but sometimes I've had ham from Gaul at my uncle's house, as a special treat, and it wasn't fat at all."

"The great thing about pigs, I always say, is that you can use up every inch of them," Gaius said, "what with sausages and puddings and brawn, not to speak of the liver and kidneys and the stomach. Tell me now, did you ever eat Trojan Pig at your uncle the Senator's house? When we were in Parthia, the Emperor was always talking about this marvellous dish, how

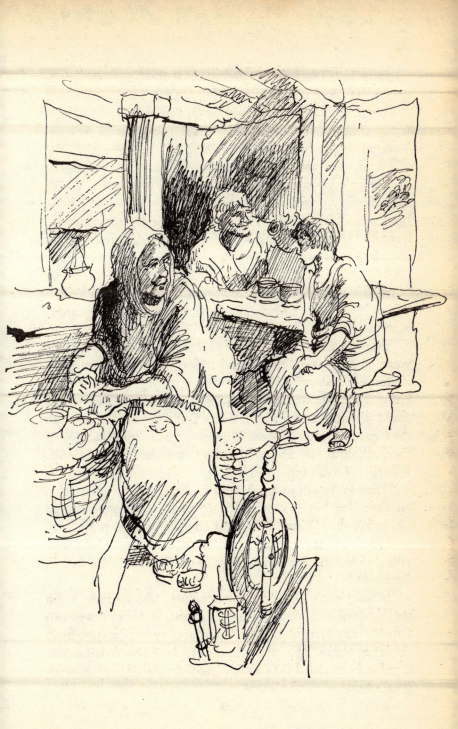

much he loved it, and how he'd have it again the first day he got back to Rome. Trojan Pig, he called it."

"No. I've heard of it, of course, but my father won't have fancy dishes in the house and I never happened to be there when they were having it at my uncle's."

"Well, the army cooks said to the Emperor's cooks one day: 'Can't you hear that poor man bleating about Trojan Pig? How can you be so hard-hearted as not to make it for him, whatever in Hades it is? If we could do it ourselves, we'd have done it for him long ago.' 'It's not the kind of thing you can do on the march,' they said, as grand as you please. '*Who's* on the march?' our cooks said. 'You lazy so-and-sos never saw a march in your lives. Get in there and make that Trojan Pig for the General or you won't do much more marching!'

"Frightened the wits out of them, they did, and off they went and cooked this awful thing—the pig's stomach, stuffed with sausages, roast chicken, eggs, vegetables—I don't know what else. It turned my stomach, though I thought I could face any food under the sun. But you should have seen the General's face—his eyes lit up, and a huge smile came over him, all slow and sort of reverent, and he said in a half-whisper: 'Trojan Pig, by Jupiter!'

"Then he began to laugh, and he said to his adjutant, that was standing beside him watching every move he made, as he always did: 'Titus, I'm going to tell you something very useful: if you say a thing often enough, someone will hear you. I didn't ask for Trojan Pig, and yet here it is. Bring in the cooks!'

"In they came, bowing and scraping, and he gave them some sort of an honour, whatever it was, and they never said a word, they were so nervous of what they had escaped from the army cooks. Then the Emperor said: 'From now on, this is going to be called 'Trajan Pig,' not 'Trojan Pig'. That was a great evening."

"I've never heard it called 'Trajan Pig'," Tullius said cautiously, after Gaius had had time to laugh himself to a standstill.

"No. It didn't take on. You can't really say 'Pig' and the Emperor's name in one breath. You won't find what I've just told you in any of the history books, but that's how it always is: history is not what happened, but what people think should have happened or may have happened. My nephew, the clever one, the one that can read, told me some of the things he has read about campaigns I was on myself, sights I saw with these two eyes, and they'd make a cat laugh."

"Wha tsort of things?"

"Oh, the strategy of battles, the routes we took—that sort of thing. But let's get back to those pigs. They're used for the sacrifice too—that's always a useful outlet. Your father, now, with his devotion to Ceres—he uses up a lot of sows, a sow for every grain crop on the farm. And we'd have the manure for the olives and the vines. The more I think about pigs instead of slaves, the better I like the idea. It could be the start of a new life for us. When we get rich, we could buy a few oxen and breed them too. I've always heard there's more money in animals and poultry than in growing corn crops and vegetables."

Tullius went home at noon with a strong feeling that he had done a good day's work. Melvia gave him a present of a honey-comb to eat on the long ride home and Gaius said:

"Be sure to come again soon, so that we can talk about those pigs. It's funny how my heart always warms to pigs."

Enumees had been waiting all this time with the horses. Part of his job consists in accompanying Tullius everywhere he goes. Sometimes he enjoys it but today he was bored because there was no one educated enough to be good company at Gaius's farm.

Though Tullius has been talking enthusiastically about

keeping pigs, he knows that the work of his own herd will be done by Hector, supervised by Scrofa, and that he will only be expected to take an interest. This will leave him plenty of time for what he really wants to do, which is to breed horses. When he broached the idea first, Decius said that he was much too young to have such valuable animals in his charge but Tullius has been working on him and noticed lately that he was softening a little. Decius has never bred horses, saying that mules are more useful and sheep the easiest to live with.

He is irritated, however, as a good Roman, by the way his friends talk of foreign horses with such respect—Huns and Burgundians, Spanish and Gaulish—anything with four legs that is not Italian will be praised. Tullius has told his father about his last visit to Rome, when his cousin Lucius brought him down to the stables to look at the horses. They were such elegant creatures, he longed to own one in particular, a Spanish stallion of noble stock, ridden by Flavius' jockey Aurelius in five races and always a winner. Decius growled:

"That young scamp Lucius will turn into a gambler, at the rate he's going."

"Not at all," said Tullius. "He never bets. He just loves to watch the horses and the chariot races."

"That's good news. Horses are a useful stock for a farmer, undoubtedly, but I wonder if they would do well here in Tibur. Before you start out on something new, it's well to find out what the traditions are. It would be no use going to a lot of expense just to breed second-rate stock."

"But I believe we could breed first-rate horses in Italy," Tullius said eagerly. "Here in Tibur we have the perfect conditions for them. We have plenty of open pasture, with good grass for most of the year, because of being near the mountains. We have the Anio river for water—that never fails. The weather is never too cold, so they could be kept in the open almost all the year round. We have plenty of room for stabling when it's cold, and we always have enough hay for winter fodder."

"You talk like a seasoned horse-breeder," Decius said. "Horses are very delicate animals. Did Lucius tell you that?"

"Of course every horse would have a slave," Tullius said, "and we'd learn how to care for them. Aurelius has a son of fourteen or so—perhaps we could get him from Uncle Flavius to start off with. Lucius says he's just like his father, that he's almost able to talk to the horses. I've seen him in the stables, rubbing them down with warm oil and covering them with blankets and giving them drinks. And Lucius says he's a genius with the foals. That's his main job at present, to stay with them when they're separated from the mares, to see that they're not frightened. And then they let him ride them when the time comes, because they know him so well."

"If he's such a genius, Flavius may not want to give him up."

"He has plenty more like him."

"And Flavius is very generous, indeed," said Decius. "Well, I'll talk to him about it and see what he says. The great drawback in horse-breeding is that you have to wait a long time for a return on your money. You can't start training high-quality horses until they're two years old, three if they're to be used for racing. And you need such a lot of space. Of course I have that piece of land up at Anticoli, that I've been using for the mules. That would be a good place for horses in summer-time, and they could harden their hooves on the mountains. My mules always do well, I must say. Yes, horses would be an interesting experiment."

"You know a lot about them, Father," said Tullius with respect.

"A farmer has to know something about everything," Decius said. "When I went into mules first, when I was not much older than you are now, I spent a couple of months up in Reate where they breed the best mules and donkeys in Italy. If you really want to go into horse-breeding, I could arrange something like that for you. There's nothing like working with an expert, seeing what he deos every day. But first we must get the pig scheme under way."

After his visit to Gaius, when Tullius reaches home he finds the whole household asleep. The sun is strong today but it is never unbearably hot up here in the hills. Still, Decius insists that everyone must lie down and restore his energies for at least an hour after the midday meal. He likes fat slaves who eat and sleep well, saying that they are less quarrelsome and troublesome than the thin kind. Knowing this, any fat slave who doesn't feel the need of a sleep makes sure to pretend to snore if Decius happens to take a stroll around the place.

Tullius takes some bread and cheese from the dining-room and then steps quietly across the compound to his bedroom, for a rest, leaving his horse to be put up by Eumenes. He has been asleep only a few minutes when the bustle outside wakens him up again, and he springs out of bed to take part in supervising the afternoon's work.

On three afternoons a week, the big, flat mule-carts are brought around to the end of the compound and loaded with produce for the market in Rome. The Emperor extended his new market near the Forum a short time ago so that it now contains one hundred and fifty little shops, on five storeys. On the ground floor there are booths for fruit and flowers, conveniently near the fountains, because the flowers have to be sprinkled with water every hour or so to keep them fresh. The first floor consists of long, vaulted halls where oil and wine are sold from the huge barrels where they are stored. A tube syphons them off into the customers' jars. Pepper and spices are sold on the second and third floors, brought there by the Indian and Arab merchants who come with trains of pack-mules from those distant countries. The spices are very important in Roman cooking, to disguise the bad smell and taste of food that has begun to go off, especially in the summer. On the fourth floor is the big hall where free issues of corn or vouchers for money are given out to the citizens of Rome.

The top floor is given over to fish-ponds, for both fresh-water and salt-water fish. Channels link the fresh-water tanks with the aqueducts, and the sea fish are kept in tanks full of water brought from the sea at Ostia.

From the top floor of the market, there is a magnificent view of the Emperor's new Forum, which is not yet finished. Slaves have been busy at it for the last year, and it is said that two more years will go by before it can be inaugurated. There will be an imposing entrance, with a portico supported by a single row of columns, and a double row of columns at either side. Beyond them will be a huge semi-circle of stone faced with marble, and in the middle a statue of the Emperor on horseback, all in gilded bronze, with statues of some of his generals and of some of the orators of former times. The building was begun by Domitian, the proud, touchy Emperor who was murdered in 96, fourteen years ago, after he had terrorised everyone for several years. Nerva, the Emperor after him, died within a year and a half, and he was too busy tidying up after Domitian to think of getting any building done. One thing he made sure of was that this good man, Trajan, should succeed him, and a very wise choice it was.

Trajan's full name is Marcus Ulpius Traianus. His mother was Spanish and he was born in Spain, so he knows that part of the Roman Empire very well indeed. He doesn't care much for show, and he thinks of his new Forum as a monument to the men who helped him to build up the Empire in Dacia. What he does care about is learning and scholarship, so the Forum is going to have two libraries, one for Greek and one for Latin books. There will also be a Basilica, which is to be called the Basilica Ulpia, and there is to be a huge column, carved in a spiral all the way to the top, with scenes illustrating the Dacian campaign.

Tullius was at the market one day with his father when they

happened to meet the architect Apollodorus, a Greek from Damascus. Decius had met him at Pliny's house, and it was he who explained the plan of the market and told them exactly how the column is going to be done. The base will be a cube, and on that will be laid seventeen cylinders of stone, each a little narrower than the one below it, so that the column will taper off as it goes up. It will be hollow inside, with forty-three windows to light it, and it will be one hundred and twenty-eight feet high. There will be a spiral staircase of one hundred and eighty-five steps inside, in white marble, and the entrance to it will be by a bronze gate. There will be a bronze eagle on top of the column, and the people on the top storey of the market will be able to look that eagle exactly in the eye.

Apollodorus said that the Emperor loves working on these plans and is himself composing the inscription which will be above the door. This will say that the purpose in erecting the column is two-fold: firstly to commemorate his victory over the distant enemies of Rome, and secondly to symbolise his victory over nature, in terracing and clearing the site for the Forum and market between the Quirinal Hill and the Capitoline Hill. The buildings are being placed so well that they will be quite in harmony with each other, and with the older Forum a short distance away.

"And it's true," Apollodorus said, "that he's doing a lot of the mathematical calculation himself. He has a genius for that sort of work—most Emperors only know how to slap a few pounds of gold here and there on a building, but he knows how it all stands up. And he's so polite—he's always careful to ask my opinion, even when he has already made up his mind what he wants to do, as I can see very well. He's a really great man."

The Basilica itself is going to be a magnificent sight, raised a yard or so above the level of the ground, with three yellow marble steps leading up to it. The floor will be white marble from Luna, and will be divided into five naves, each a hundred and fifty yards long, the middle one being wider than the others. There will be ninety-six pillars dividing the naves, and there will be room for a great many statues between the pillars of the portico outside. The two libraries will be built one at either side of the column, on the terrace above the Basilica, so that they can all be seen from the Forum below. There are to be busts of the best Greek and Latin writers on top of the cupboards containing the books.

Looking down from the market, none of this magnificence can yet be guessed at. All that can be seen is a mass of scurrying slaves, moving blocks of stone, clearing away rubble, digging out new foundations, constantly beaten and ordered about by screaming overseers, who have developed a knack of hardening their voices to make them more insistent. Already the shopkeepers in the market complain that they have headaches by the end of the day, from the noise of hammering and yelling that goes on from dawn to dusk below them.

All this excitement is a world away from the quiet farm in Tibur, where Regulus the slave manager is organising the loading of the carts to go to Rome. Regulus never shouts, saying that one would have to shout louder every day of one's life, if one were to be logical, because people only heed a voice that is louder than usual. He hurries the other slaves by darting about among them like a sheep-dog, lending a hand here and there with a heavy basket, or lifting a few small ones himself and heaving them on to a cart.

The baskets are made of willow rods for heavy vegetables and fruit, and of dried reeds for lettuce and spinach and herbs and garlic. They are made by the slaves in the winter-time, when there is not much farm work to do, and are stacked in a great pile to last through the summer. The willow baskets often last for several seasons but the lighter ones are quickly worn out.

The carts are long, with four wheels, and are pulled by one

or by two mules according to their size. Regulus likes to keep them well painted, and he sees that their silver decorations and the silver bells and trappings on the harness are always kept polished. He gets the cleverer slaves to decorate the paint-work with flowers and birds and fruit, and has a reputation in all Latium for the beauty of his carts.

Today there are several loads of vegetables and fruit. The apricots and cherries are in, and there is a whole cartload of each, lying softly on beds of their own leaves. When they are loaded, Regulus covers them with a little straw and then some more leaves, to keep the flies off. Then there are baskets of cabbage and sprouting broccoli and onions and lettuce, and a very precious few baskets of small marrows, just ready for sale and likely to get a good price tomorrow in the market.

Another cart carries only cheeses, the soft, white, curdy one made from sheep's milk, the rolls of sharp-tasting goat's cheese with a thick yellow rind, the smooth, round, pale-yellow cow's milk cheese with a thin straw rope tied around its neck so that it looks like a little bottle, and the squashy, snow-white cheese made from the milk of the big white oxen that pull the carts in the fields. These last have to be kept in bowls of their own whey, to keep them fresh, and they splash and squelch all the way to the City.

Next come baskets of tiny birds, packed close together, plucked and cleaned. Getting them ready has taken since this hour yesterday, when the slave in charge of the poultry collected them in nets from the aviary and twisted their necks one by one and threw them to the women slaves to pluck. They sat up all night at it, working by the light of oil-lamps, because in this hot weather all meat begins to go off at once, and birds seem specially vulnerable.

There are baskets of chickens as well, but they have been ready since last night, and so have the peacocks. There are special, long baskets that go on the same carts, to take the tail feathers which are so highly valued as decoration.

Plucking peacocks is a job for a very experienced slave indeed, and Regulus stands over the man while he is working at it, to make sure that none of the feathers are spoiled. The little breast feathers of the cocks are kept apart, and Lavinia has been teaching Clodia how to make fans of them by sticking them in rows on an ivory base.

One cart carries only live lambs, and another has baskets of eggs.

With such delicate cargo, the mule-carts must travel slowly, since the road to Rome is very rough. After rain, parts of it are a mass of greyish mud and later, when the sun has baked the mud dry, there are always deep ruts made by the wheels of the carts. Every step is dangerous, especially on the steeper parts of the road, but the drivers are very skilled and experienced. They know every inch of the way and are quick to see if the surface has been altered by the weather. Then they send a man out in front to navigate for the whole line.

They start off about an hour before midnight. It's delightfully cool then, with plenty of light in the sky though there is no moon. Still, each cart carries a lantern swinging from one shaft. There has been no rain for some time, and though it's good that there is no mud, the cart-wheels raise a cloud of fine dust which follows them, coating men and beasts and their loads with silver-grey. As they wind down the long hills one by one, they see the City in the plain below them huddled like a huge dog asleep. From all the hills around, trains of mules are moving down, their lanterns showing a flickering light now and then as they turn this way or that.

Hours ago, soon after dark, Tullius and Clodia, Decius and Lavinia, Eumenes and Regulus and all the household slaves retired to bed and are fast asleep. All night long, until the first light wakens Regulus and he begins to rouse the other slaves, the big grey dogs of the farm pace round and round the compound, guarding it from the wolves that prowl the hills by night.

CHAPTER FOUR

A Stall-holder's Family

When the train of carts arrives at the market at three o'clock in the morning, Quintus is waiting beside his father, Lepidus, at the stall. Lepidus is the brother of Regulus, the slave manager of Decius' farm. He was once a slave himself, in the household of Flavius the Senator, but he was freed years ago when he married and set up a stall in the market with the money he had saved up. This was the natural thing for him to do: when he worked for Flavius, his job was to take care of the fruit and vegetables that were delivered to the house, both from the gardens and from Decius' country estate. He had a big store-room under his charge, with three other slaves to help him keep it. He has three helpers now too—his wife, Licinia, his son, Quintus, who is fifteen, and his daughter, Antonia, who is twelve.

When Lepidus married Licinia he was thinking of his little stall, and he has proved very wise in this. She was a slave too, in the garland-room, and she became an expert at making wreaths to be worn at dinner-parties, and all sorts of garlands for decoration. She is training Antonia in the same skill, and they are so good at it that they are bringing lots of customers to the stall.

Quintus doesn't look like an Italian, in spite of his Roman name. His parents were both born and brought up in

Flavius' house but Lepidus' father was Egyptian. Licinia has heard that her mother was a Gaul but no one is quite certain about this, nor who her father was. When she was small, she was often told that she was lucky to be alive at all, as girl babies were often thrown out on the rubbish dump. People are beginning to think that this is not quite right, yet they still do it. Neither Flavius nor his father ever allowed such a thing to happen in their households.

Last night, from seven o'clock when darkness fell, Quintus slept with the rest of the family on a woollen mattress on the floor. They have a room in Serpent Street, beside the market, on the third floor of a four-storey house. The smell in their room is devastating, not only from the crowded conditions but also from the cess-pit under the stairs which is used by all the tenants to empty their chamber-pots and slop-buckets. No one in their senses would spend a moment longer than necessary at home.

Quintus slept in his clothes, a loin-cloth and a linen tunic, so all he had to do was tie the thongs of his sandals around his ankles and get out into the street as fast as possible. On the way to the market, he filled his lungs deliberately over and over again, with fresh air.

Other families have already arrived at the market by the time he gets there. They must start the day very early, to get things in order before the first customers come. Everything will be closed down in the afternoon so that they can all go to the baths, and the prospect of the fun they will have there with their friends makes the hard day's work well worth while.

When the first cart comes in, Quintus lifts the baskets of flowers down and lays them carefully at the back of the stall, where they will be safe from trampling feet. His mother and his sister keep a close eye on them. He turns back to help his father unload the other things. Trestle tables, tilted towards the front, make a fine display of the baskets of fruit. Lepidus places them himself, turning the best side of each piece outwards.

At the next stall, jealous old Octavian is casting sidelong glances at them. He is a thin little man with greyish hair, going bald, and a permanently anxious expression. He has his little boy, Marcellus, with him, the last of the family, twelve years old, already with the same anxious look on his face that his father has. Marcellus always makes a point of looking very busy, as if to suggest that he and his father have so many customers that they can hardly attend to the tidying up. If he has a basket to carry, he holds it high and pretends to stagger with the weight of it. At other times he darts up and down, touching the goods, rearranging them very slightly, sometimes calling out:

"Oh, how lovely! Oh, such cherries! Oh, such apricots!"

Sometimes this brings a woman away from a neighbouring stall, and then Marcellus becomes wildly excited, weighing her fruit so often that he gets several different results, dropping some on the ground, putting in a piece that she has rejected as having gone off. More than once, Quintus has seen poor Marcellus get a cuff on the ear for his incompetence.

Fortunately the neighbour with the stall beyond Octavian's is very good-humoured. He doesn't sell fancy stuff and he keeps his prices down, so he is never short of a certain kind of customer. He is called Demetrius, which is a Greek name, but he certainly does not look like a Greek. He is very tall and thin, with wild black hair and a huge mouthful of teeth which have been repaired with bits of gold. He says that he had this done in Puteoli by a local dentist but no one really believes him. They think he was probably in North Africa with some pirates, and doesn't want to be questioned about his doings there. Where would a poor man find the money for gold teeth otherwise? He loves to show them off, with a wide and gleaming smile. Now and then he walks towards Octavian's stall and chants:

"Octavian's going backwards, I go forwards!"

Octavian turns his shoulder to him and gets very busy with his fruit but Marcellus calls out loudly:

"Oh, how beautiful! Oh, such cherries! Oh, such a colour!"

At the back of the stall, Licinia and Antonia are already busy making decorations. Licinia has a stock of willow rods standing against the wall, and she takes two or three of them and twists them into a ring or into a tall oval shape. She covers these with moss, patting and pushing it in between the rods, turning in the ends and plaiting them together firmly so that they won't come undone when they are moved. She has laurel leaves to cover the moss, for the wreaths that are meant to last longer. Laurel doesn't fade nor go soft for weeks, and all kinds of flowers can be stuck in among the leaves to liven them up, at the last moment.

Some of the wreaths are made in the shape of a doorway,

ready to be attached to doorposts or to be erected as an archway for the guests to walk under as they enter the house.

Most troublesome to make are the wreaths that must be placed on the heads of guests when they arrive for dinner. The flowers must be small and delicate to look at, but tough and hard-wearing enough to last out an evening, or at least as long as the company is sober enough to notice their condition. When she is making them, Licinia tries to imagine the face of some fine, dignified guest, Pliny, perhaps, who is worth decorating. The dining-room slaves have told her that he wears his wreath with an air, never lets it fall askew nor get trampled underfoot as some of the others do.

When she was new to the work, Licinia wept when she heard how her lovely wreaths finished the evening but now she just concentrates on presenting them as beautifully as she can. Their wearers can be as piggy as they like afterwards.

Today she has roses and tiny, sweet-smelling lilies, both good for twelve hours after they leave her hands. As a frame for them, she uses the lightest twig of willow, and she doesn't attach the flowers to them until she knows exactly when they will be needed. This morning there are four banquets to be provided for, the biggest with twenty-seven people at it. Antonia and Licinia will need the whole morning to get the wreaths ready for delivery by noon, and they must dart in and out to the counter as well, if Quintus and Lepidus are busy.

Not much cooking is done in Rome, since most people live on bread and cheese and fruit. Vegetables are mostly eaten raw, and any cooking that is done is managed on charcoal stoves which are always liable to set fire to the wooden floors of the apartments. Because of this, and the smell at home, Licinia prefers to do her cooking at the market, and she keeps a little stove there on which she can make soup or boil a chicken or some of the sacrificial meat, if she can get it.

By four o'clock the stall is laid out with all the things that Lepidus has for sale and the buyers from the rich people's houses have begun to arrive. These well-off slaves are very arrogant and demanding, much worse than their masters. They are practising for the day when they will be free and able to own slaves of their own. Some don't want to be free at all, but these are the clerks and stewards of the Emperor, what we would call civil servants, and they have almost as much power as the Emperor himself, though they keep in the background.

Quintus doesn't want to have a stall in the market like his father, when he is older. He would like to do better, and he can see that there are many ways in which he can get rich if he puts his mind to it. Both Marcus and Flavius noticed him when he was small and remarked that he was a bright boy, and said that they would help him in any way they could when he was older. This is a wonderful thing for Quintus—patronage of this kind is the most important thing in a Roman's life. He knows he is clever, because he learned to read and write so easily when he went to school. He is very grateful to his father for having sent him there, though it was a horrible experience, and he knows that Lepidus had a hard time collecting the few pence that he had to pay the teacher each week.

At first it was rather exciting to go at dawn to the tent where the school was held, outside a shop in Pepper Street. The tent was attached to the wall of the shop and hung down to the ground, but it could not keep out the noises that went on up and down the street—shouts of pedlars, arguments, greetings, jokes told with shrieks of laughter, slapping of slaves' feet as they carried their masters along in litters, horses' hooves, all became blended into a confusing roar that made his head spin, so that after a week or two he begged his father to let him go to work in the stall instead.

"I know it's dreadful," Lepidus said, "but if you can't read and write, you'll be a nobody all your life. The other children can put up with it—you should be able to do the same. Even the girls don't complain."

"They're afraid, that's why," said Quintus. "That master is a walking devil. Not a minute passes that he doesn't beat someone."

"Perhaps they're disobedient, peeking out on to the street, chattering to each other, playing games under the desk—"

"Some of them are doing those things but he doesn't need a reason to beat us. He counts on his fingers, up to four, then he asks: 'Can everyone count up to four? Who can't count up to four?' And he beats a few of the boys and girls nearest to him. Then he starts again."

"If this goes on, you'll be able to count up to four, and up to fourteen," Lepidus pointed out. "You're eight years old now. By the time you're twelve, you'll be able to figure and read and write, three things I've always wanted to do."

"By the time I'm twelve, that man will have been the death of me," said Quintus, and he would have liked to add that if his father was so fixed on learning, he should have a taste of it himself and all the things that went with it. But he didn't dare to say that.

As time went on, however, he learned how to sit as far away from the master as possible, which saved him to some extent. And he did learn to read and write and add and subtract and multiply, through hearing everything repeated over and over again until he thought the boredom of it would drive him mad. It never did: but he often thought that there must surely be another way to teach small children these things than to yell them into their ears over and over, for four or five or even six years.

When he was twelve, he went one day with Lepidus to Senator Flavius' house, and the great man spoke to him for several minutes, questioning him about what he was learning. Then he said:

"When you are well able to read, you can come sometimes and look at the books in my library. Would you like that?"

"Yes, sir, indeed I would," Quintus said, "but I can read only Latin and I think most of your books are in Greek."

"Ah, yes, that is true," Flavius said vaguely. "Learn Greek, then, and come and read them."

But Quintus knows that he'll never have time to do this, though his children may, if he does well.

Quintus has been to the huge store-houses near the Tiber, beyond the Emperor's palace, where mountains of goods from all over the Empire are kept—wood and building materials, painted tiles and bricks, lead, silver and copper, papyrus for making books, porphyry and alabaster, salt and dried meat, gold and tin, precious stones and marbles, glass

143

and coral, wool, oil, corn, spices and incense, fine silk and cotton, leather and ivory. Rich and poor use all these things, and the businessmen who handle them get a rake-off on every ounce that they sell to the shopkeepers. Marcus keeps a lot of his stock there.

Not only the thought of the fortune waiting to be picked up, but the excitement of all those smells and colours make the store-houses Quintus' favourite place in all Rome. The history of the whole Empire is there, from Rome in a great circle that takes in Britain and Spain and North Africa and Egypt and Dacia and Bithynia and India and Germany. Rome is the mistress of the whole world, and the whole world has to pay tribute to her. It's a great thing to be a citizen of Rome, and only a fool would spend all his life serving when he might command.

He would begin in a small way, naturally. The important thing is to pick a business that is not a dead end. Tradesmen, for instance, are liable to get stuck at their work, as his uncle Publius has told him. Publius is a barber, not exactly a tradesman perhaps, but certainly a man tied to his shop from day to day in such a way that he will never have time to expand. He's happy enough, however, so long as he makes enough money to go to the baths and have a day out at the circus or a festival, and so long as none of his regular customers fall out with him.

Quintus has to go to the barber once a week now, and soon he will have to go every other day for a shave. He doesn't look forward to that, remembering how Publius' customers usually come out with a few bloody nicks in their faces from the blunt razor. The daily shave is a necessity for most of the older men and the chance to meet and chat with their friends for half an hour makes up for the blood. Quintus does not want to be a barber, though Publius would take him on as an apprentice if he did.

Most of the other trades would be just as bad, swallowing

up his life so that he would suddenly find that he was old and had nothing to show for it. His father didn't like to hear him talk like this when they had a conversation about it a few weeks ago.

"It's an honourable thing to be a tradesman," Lepidus said. "And who wants to be rich anyway? Look at what happens to the rich from time to time: there they were, all flocking around Domitian when he was the Emperor, afraid to stay away from his levées lest he might notice their absence and be offended, afraid to go lest he might notice their presence and have them executed for some insult, real or imaginary."

Quintus pointed out that he didn't want to be rich or important enough to be noticed by the Emperor at all. All he wants is to have a big flat like Marcus'—the old flat, not the new house—and to have slaves of his own and a litter for going to the Colosseum and the Circus Maximus and the baths.

"A litter! Slaves!" Lepidus was scandalised. "You'll defy the gods!"

"Not at all. I've kept my ears open and I've heard you and your friends speak often of how poor men have got on in the world. With proper saving, some day I might have enough money to belong to the Equestrian Order—"

"Praise be to Jupiter! And when will that be?"

"Fate will decide. Then I'll have you and Mother to live with me and advise my wife—"

"Oh, so you're married now. You're moving very fast. Perhaps your wife won't want to be advised by us."

"She'll want it, all right. I'll have a special seat in the theatre, and I'll be on the Juries, and I'll make money out of collecting taxes in the colonies."

"Good luck to you. When are you going to begin?"

"I thought you could ask Marcus to give me a start, now that I'm good at figures."

"A very good idea. I saw you the other day, figuring up

145

Marcus' account in two shakes, multiplying by one figure instead of adding up the same number over and over again as most people have to do. You're a bright boy, and no mistake. Well, I'll talk to Marcus and see what he has to say. His grandfather was a slave in Flavius' house, so he knows what it's like to be poor."

Lepidus did talk to Marcus, who has said that he will give Quintus a job in one of his offices at the end of the summer, and that in the meantime he is to help his father as much as he can. With this prospect to look forward to, Quintus is glad to work extra hard. He is almost ashamed to admit to himself that he admires Marcus more than he does Flavius, who is far more cultivated and far more educated. It's the businessmen who really matter in the Empire, and Quintus has heard people say that Flavius and his fellow Senators are gradually going to be less powerful.

When the flow of customers begins to die down, Quintus takes two big rush baskets and fills them with onions and lettuce and cabbage to sell to the housewives who have not been able to come to the market. He chooses light-weight things because he may have to carry them a long distance. This is the only way in which goods can be transported around the City, since Julius Caesar's decree against carts and beasts of burden. From sunrise to sunset these are not allowed to move in the City, and any that came in during the night and were not out by the dawn have to stand where they are throughout the day following. Five exceptions are permitted: the chariots of the Vestal Virgins, who are given many privileges out of respect; the chariot of the Rex Sacrorum, the priest who now performs the sacrifices that used to be looked after by the king in former times; the chariots that are used for the games on game days; and the chariots that are used for Triumphs. The fifth kind of vehicle allowed in Rome by day is the builder's cart, either with its heavy battering-ram for knocking down burned-out houses, or loaded with building materials. This hot June morning, it seems to Quintus that there is one of these in every street, sending rubble and masonry flying through the air so that he has to duck out of the way, filling his lungs with dust, threatening to break his legs with stretched ropes and beams sticking out of the backs of the carts or with blocks of marble which seem always on the point of falling off them.

He stops for a while to watch Marcus' slaves at work. They have brought the ram into position opposite a block of flats in Serpent Street, a few doors up from his own block, and have erected a scaffold for it so that it is on a level with the top storey. Up there, six slaves are ranged three at either side, with the ram swinging between them. Back and forth, back and forth it goes, each time nearer to the wall of the building. Then it begins to strike it, harder and harder, until at last it makes a hole. The slaves shift it slightly so that it touches the wall at another point. Now the whole wall is tottering. A crowd has gathered, their mouths wide open to gaze upwards. The wall gives a shiver and topples slowly into the street while the gazers skip out of the way.

Quintus is thinking that it would surely be a better bargain to build a house that would last, rather than another ramshackle one like this. But Marcus won't do that, though he knows how to build well, as can be seen by the house he built for himself. Quintus passes it by on his way up the hill, a solid, comfortable house with a beautiful garden and orchard around it. He quickens his steps, to get his cabbages sold.

He turns into narrow alleys leading one from another, now and then pausing to yell at the top of his voice:

"I have fine lettuce and onions and cabbage for you, woman of the house! Come out, come down and see what I have! Lettuce grown by my own uncle Regulus, in Tibur, on the banks of the Anio!" He stretches out the syllables and makes his voice echo off the walls. "Come down and see my onions! Come down and see my cabbage!"

From the top of a three-storey building, a woman pops her head out of the window and calls out:

"Wait there, boy, and I'll come down!"

He waits in the middle of the street because once, a year ago, he saw a man with fruit to sell, who had shouted too loud for comfort, drenched from head to foot by a furious woman from an upstairs window. She had thrown the contents of a chamber-pot on to him, and when he called the police and complained about her, she could not be found. The policeman pointed out that according to the law, if anyone threw a chamber-pot or its contents out of the

window, the responsibility rested on all the other tenants of the floor from which it was thrown. Quintus never found out whether they all had to pay up, but he had learned a lesson he never forgot.

This time he is safe enough. Several women come and buy from him, grumbling at the price as usual, but on the whole pleased enough with what he has brought. He tells them, truly, that he is not charging any more than if they went to the market themselves, and they call other women to pass on the good news. One of them says:

"If what you say is true, then you can come again to-morrow and we'll all be waiting for you. Isn't that so, girls?"

The "girls" are all little round fat women old enough to be his grandmother. They agree that if he keeps his prices down, they will give him their custom. Soon he moves on, having made a good beginning on his career as a businessman.

With empty baskets he comes back to the market and hands the money to his father, who says:

"Now go across to the Forum and find out if Diocles the Greek has got those sandals ready for me. I pay good prices but if I were a rich man he would have sent his son running to me with them a week ago. Now I have to send mine running to him."

Quintus is delighted with an excuse to go to the Forum and sets off immediately. He makes for the stalls at once, strolling along slowly so as to see all the things on display. He is specially interested in the jewellery stalls, because he knows that Marcus buys precious stones in India as well as gold to set them in. He also buys finished rings and bracelets and hair ornaments made in India, but most Roman women like the finer Roman settings better. He sells his gold to the cameo-makers for the elegant frames that they put on their brooches and pendants, and elephant tusks from Africa to the ivory-carvers, for making combs and ornaments as well as figures of gods and heroes of all sizes.

Quintus would like to learn all about that side of Marcus' business and hopes that he will be allowed to do so after a while. He knows that Marcus' son Gallus is not interested in business and that Marcus himself is more concerned with his bigger projects, like tax-collecting and lending money to the Government. It could well happen that an intelligent clerk who took the trouble to find out every detail of the jewellery trade might become a very valuable person indeed. Of all types of business, it lent itself most to the depredations of dishonest employees, so Quintus would make sure to deserve a reputation for honesty. Eventually Marcus might help him to start up on his own, a distant dream but not a ridiculous one.

He stops at a stall where a very bent, thin man is working at making a pearl necklace. He is picking up the pearls one by one with a pair of tweezers, screwing up his eyes to see that he has the right size of pearl, threading it on a silk string and knotting the string at either side of it. Already his eyesight is affected by such close, exact work—none of that for Quintus. Beside him is a mirror shop, with mirrors of all sizes ranged around the walls and some hanging up outside. There are mirrors for hanging on walls, with elaborate carved frames, animals and birds and flowers, and some plain ones as well. Some of the frames are covered with gold. There are hand-mirrors with silver or gold frames, some decorated with pearls from the shop next door.

The mirrors are made of polished metal from various mines both in Italy and in other parts of the Empire. With the sun glistening on them there in the spruce shop in the Forum, no one would guess at the pain and labour it took to get that metal above ground. The work is so horrible that it's quite usual to have it done by condemned criminals or slaves. Even the engineers and overseers are slaves, who can't go on strike or leave the job when it becomes intolerable. In some of the mines, the workers are never allowed to come above ground at all, lest they might refuse to go below again later.

The galleries in the mines are very narrow, because the Romans have not found out that mines can be propped while in use or packed with sand when they have been worked out. Boys are sent creeping along these galleries carrying trays of ore, and they often smother for lack of air because the candles they carry use up the oxygen. Another danger is from flooding, though various drainage pumps have been invented and are used in bigger mines. These pumps have to be worked constantly by slaves, and a poor man working a small mine on his own couldn't afford enough of them to keep a pump going. The big mines are owned by the state and are not short of money. Some of them have a new kind of waterwheel which can operate to a depth of seventy-five yards, and long channels have been made through the rock to drain the water away.

Iron is the hardest metal to mine and gold the easiest, though it is much scarcer. The gold in the rivers in Gaul only has to be panned out. The Emperor's latest conquests in Dacia have been wonderfully valuable because there are huge gold-fields there, so much that it may no longer be worth while bringing gold from the mines in Spain and Greece. One of the difficulties about gold is that it is poisonous, like lead, and the miners die in dozens underground, from breathing in the vapours it gives off.

Beyond the mirror shop there is a druggist and perfume seller, and most of his wares are made from very peculiar materials indeed. For ointments to cure rashes he makes an infusion of ants, with their nest, or one made from the excrement of cats, which he also uses for making perfume. He burns lead and pounds it up in vinegar, to be used as an ointment against madness, but he warns his customers not to drink it as the lead is poisonous.

For fits he has cures made of herbs, fruits and flowers which he has gathered on a day favoured by the gods—

elder-flowers, willow leaves, rose hips, lily of the valley, castor leaves, lemons, mint and radishes.

For curing nose-bleeds he keeps live toads, which the patient must hold under his armpits. For headaches he has a concoction of pigeon's dung, salt, radish roots and vinegar to be applied to the soles of the feet and the palms of the hands. Pliny's uncle put a great deal of information about plants that could be used as medicines into his book on natural history, and the druggist knows this book very well and constantly refers to it.

The drug shop is only used for minor illnesses. Anyone who is really sick calls in a Greek doctor or, if he is rich, keeps one permanently in the house. Flavius has one called Micon who is expert in the ideas of Hippocrates and was taught by Dioscorides Pedanus, Nero's doctor.

Like his teacher, Micon has no time for superstition, for amulets inscribed with prayers to be worn around the neck of the sick person, or dedication of models of the affected parts of the body to the appropriate gods. He goes to work scientific-ally, yet he agrees with the great Hippocrates that you can't separate the causes of disease into purely natural and purely spiritual: all disease has both divine and human elements and each must be given its proper amount of consideration. He believes that the human body is made up of four cardinal fluids, or humours: blood, phlegm, yellow bile and black bile. When the person is well, his humours are blended harmoni-ously; when he is ill, it is because they are in disharmony. Sick people are cured by restoring the natural harmony of the humours, and this is best brought about by natural means.

The first thing to be done, then, is to find out how the patient normally lives, whether he habitually eats or drinks too much, whether he wears suitable clothes for the time of year, whether he travels in distant places where the climate is not healthy.

His habits are adjusted and he is made to rest and be quiet, and if he is still not well, mild cures are tried out. Barley water is a favourite one, and infusions of camomile to calm the patient down and make him sleep.

If anyone disagrees with Micon's methods and thinks he ought to do something more positive, he quotes the aphorism of his teacher: "Life is short and Art is long, the occasion is urgent, experience is deceptive and decision difficult; not only must the physician be ready to do his duty but patient, attendants and circumstances must co-operate if there is to be a cure." That usually silences everyone and leaves him free to get on with his own plans.

Micon always begins his treatment by telling the relations of the sick person what he thinks is likely to happen to him, whether he will get well soon or whether it will be a long, complicated illness, whether he will live or die. As he is very often right in his prognosis, he has a great reputation. After he has tried the effect of rest, barley water and camomile, his most usual cure is bleeding, opening a vein and letting out some of the black blood which is causing the patient's melancholy, as he says. Often the temperature goes down at once and the patient feels better. After that, herbal remedies should finish the job. If they don't, the skin can be blistered either with a hot iron or with some very irritating herb, made into an ointment. Most people stop complaining about their pains and aches after a spell of this kind of treatment.

Unknown to Micon, sometimes the sick person's friends go down to the temple to offer sacrifice to the gods for his cure. It is thought best to go to the god who specialises in the part of the body affected—the head, the limbs, the stomach and so on.

The first Greek doctors were slaves, but Julius Caesar made a decree that anyone practising medicine had to be freed. There is a medical school in Rome, founded by the Emperor Vespasian who was also very much concerned about public health. He tried to clean up the City after the

154

civil wars in 69, and put the Empire back on its feet by making sure that the taxes were collected and properly spent on reconstruction. Then he built the Colosseum and generally encouraged other cities throughout the Empire to manage their own affairs. Because of his interest, there are also medical schools in Gaul, mostly in the south.

There are state and army doctors, and many public hospitals throughout the Empire. One army doctor has created a sensation with his cure for migraine, by drilling a hole in a certain part of the patient's skull, carefully chosen. If the patient survives that, he never complains of headaches again.

Some Roman doctors know quite a lot about the structure of the human body, from dissecting both dead people and animals. They know that the heart is the most important organ in the body, and that the blood somehow produces heat, but they have not worked out that this is caused by circulation. They think that the arteries contain air, because in dead animals they are always empty. They know that the liver is very important and believe that it sends a "vital spirit" flowing throughout the body by means of the veins, and they even know that something happens to the venous blood which cleans it and makes it bright red instead of dark. Their biggest mistake is in thinking that the heart and not the brain is the seat of the intelligence, though they know that the brain is very important. They know a great deal about the nervous system, and believe that what they call the "animal spirit" comes from the brain and is distributed by the nerves, but as all the experiments to prove this were done on cattle, not on people, the conclusions are not accurate. Towards the end of the century, the great doctor Galen will make his discoveries by dissecting monkeys and knowledge will advance enormously.

Very few doctors have an interest in this kind of experiment or speculation—they are too busy, and besides they have a strong idea that the old cures are the most reliable. No point in relying on foolish magic when a bag of wolf's dung, hung around the patient's neck, will effect a proper cure that you can depend on.

The Greeks are excellent surgeons, and in some ways their practices differ very little from those in use in our time. This is specially true of bone surgery. They believe in keeping the operating theatre very clean and tidy, and in washing the hands of the surgeon just before he goes to work, although they know nothing specific about germs. The instruments should be kept very clean too, in a special place, and the light should be good enough for the surgeon to see clearly and exactly what he is doing.

A great deal of the surgeon's experience is acquired, naturally, on the battle-field. This does not mean that it can't be used at home: directions for repairing a wound made by a sword, for instance, are that the wound should be cleaned, some blood sucked out and the edges laid together and bandaged, then a pain-killing concoction of dried herbs rubbed in and the whole area covered by an airtight bandage. This could equally well apply if the victim were a housewife who slipped and fell on the carving-knife, or a man who got involved in a knife fight in the Forum. For broken limbs and fractured skulls, some of the techniques are exactly the same as are used in our day.

Not all of the operations done are repairs of violent injuries: the surgeons know how to operate on cataracts in the eyes, and on hernias, and how to take out tonsils and polypi from the nose, and how to remove a goitre, which is a tricky business even for modern surgeons.

The great Greek surgeons who have practised in Rome are Meges and Heliodorus, and they have both written books for their students. The author of the best book on surgery of the ear, nose and throat is Aulus Cornelius Celsus, who was not a doctor at all. He lived in the time of Tiberius, almost a hundred years before the present Emperor, and had many other interests besides medicine—in fact he wrote an encyclopaedia with sections on rhetoric, philosophy, agriculture and military science, as well as on medicine. For all of these he had to consult experts, as no one could possibly know so many different things well, and the expert he consulted on medicine was a famous doctor named Themison, who was a friend of his. Themison was the first doctor to study chronic diseases and to write about them intelligently.

The founder of the whole medical profession was a small man named Hippocrates who lived about six hundred years before the Emperor Trajan. He was a Greek, from the island of Cos, and his name will be honoured for ever by doctors, because he set up the ethical standards of the medical profession. The oath that an apprentice doctor takes to serve his master is known as the Hippocratic Oath.

The Emperor Claudius, who reigned until the year 54, gave special status to the island of Cos, in honour of Hippocrates. Very little is known about him, but he must have been a powerful personality to have become such a legend. He travelled a lot and probably visited anyone who was trying to practise medicine, and gave them advice. He had a strong idea, which seems very sensible to us now with our knowledge of psychology, that you can't just cure the human body as if it were a piece of machinery, taking each part separately. He said that the whole body is a complete organism, with each part and function depending on the whole, and that there is no such thing as a purely mechanical illness—there is always a divine reason as well, caused by the cold, the sun and the winds. By this he seems to show that he had observed what we call the psychosomatic element in illness, which means that the mental condition of the patient may be a large factor in the progress of the disease, or even the whole cause of it. But he seems to have had no great interest in psychology, and simply believed that the gods took a hand in all the affairs of men.

The written works of this great doctor are contained in the Hippocratic Collection, but it is thought that he is not the author of all the works that come under that name. Plato, who was a contemporary of his, had a great regard for Hippocrates, and was partly responsible for laying down the code of behaviour for doctors which became the ideal one. It was part of a complex philosophy which teaches that virtue is knowledge and that wrong is only done through ignorance. Arising from this, Plato believed that the pursuit of knowledge is a good thing in itself, and that knowledge comes from teaching rather than persuasion. The human soul has three parts: the natural appetites, the spirit of free will and the spirit of reason. If all three function together, he said, you have a virtuous person. Vice will always be unhappy because it consists of disorder and disharmony between the three parts of man's nature. The natural lesson to be learned from this philosophy is that man should cultivate himself very highly and make himself an expert in his own subject, keeping himself in training for the practice of it, both mentally and physically. In the case of doctors, this will mean that a good doctor must be a virtuous, disciplined man whose whole personality will be put at the service of knowledge, and who will be incapable of acting in an unethical way. Plato believed too that government, like medicine, is a job for experts, and that a good governor should not have to fall back on the law to reinforce his decrees. That part of his theory is no longer popular.

It is no wonder that the Roman doctors are not Romans at all but Greeks, since the whole way of thinking that makes them so learned is quite different from the Roman one.

Quintus has never had any reason to be treated by a doctor, and his mother's remedies for the stomach-ache are so rough and ready that he prefers to pretend to feel well. The very smell of the druggist's shop makes him feel seedy and he hurries on past it to the shoemaker, Diocles.

Diocles makes men's sandals, which are just a flat sole of thick leather with some leather thongs to tie around the ankles. The thongs are secured through a hole drilled in the sole, one at either side, and the sandal is ready. Diocles also makes boots for riding, which come halfway up the calves of the legs and are tied across the front with thongs. These take longer, but he and his apprentice can make several dozen pairs in a day. The leather is kept at the back of the shop, great slabs of cow-skin from which they cut what they need from time to time. Diocles is not allowed to have a tannery inside the Forum because of the smell, but he has one down by the river and brings what leather he needs every day.

Quintus puts the sandals under his arm and strolls on, past a stall where beautiful silk dresses are laid out on the counter so that the ladies can finger them as they pass by. The owner is a tall, smooth-looking man with a soft voice, who sidles up to each potential customer and purrs into her ear as sweetly as a cat. If he sells a dress, he remains sweet for a good ten minutes; if the lady walks on, he turns and snarls like a dog at his wife and her sister who are sitting behind the counter embroidering wide bands on the hems of dresses. They lift their eyes and look at him indifferently for a split second, and then turn back to their work and their own conversation, which is all about babies and marriages and funerals and what the Emperor's cousin Julia wore at the games last week. The man looks so sad, it worries Quintus at first, but then he takes out a toothpick and cleans his teeth with such an intent expression that it's impossible to believe he's really sad after all.

Beyond all the shops is the house of the Vestal Virgins. Quintus knows that the moment he gets home, Antonia will ask him if he saw any of them driving out in their chariots or walking about. Quintus said to her once:

"Why do you think so much about them? I know they're very important people and we're all supposed to respect

them, but I don't hear the other girls talking about them all the time, as you do."

"I wish I were one of them!"

Quintus was shocked.

"How could you wish such a thing? To be locked up there all your life, never to be married or have children of your own, to be afraid for your life if you let the sacred fire go out—how would you like to be beaten by the Emperor? That's what happens to them, if they let anything go wrong."

"They don't let the fire go out, and I wouldn't let it go out either," Antonia said contemptuously. "One would have to be a complete ass to let such a thing happen. Besides, I'd light it up again before the Emperor found out about it. Their new house is so fine! There are fifty rooms on the ground floor, just for the six of them. One would never get tired of a house like that. There are two other floors, and they all look into a courtyard full of roses."

Quintus thinks it would be a great bore to live all one's life in such a quiet place, knowing that so many things were happening beyond the walls, but Antonia dreams of a marvellous peace, with no smells, no noise, no shouting, everything so slow and grand and dignified, everyone bowing and keeping out of the way whenever they go out. It's too late for her to be one of them now, though she could have been offered as a Vestal at any time between the ages of six and ten, if there had been a vacancy for one. Being poor and the daughter of a freedman would not have prevented it. If the Emperor chose her from among all the candidates with the wonderful words: "Te, amata, capio", "I choose thee, beloved", she would have been handed over to him and he would have taken responsibility for her from her father from then onwards. The trouble is that there are so many candidates and so few places—but at least the dream is open to all.

Once inside the house of the Vestals, her hair would be cut off and hung on a sacred lotus tree as an offering to the gods.

When the hair grew again, it would be dressed in a special way that only the Vestals used, though it was once the way that all Roman women wore theirs. It would be divided in six parts, and turned up over six pads of artificial hair, kept in place by a band with strips hanging down at either side. Then she would be dressed in long white robes, the colour and style that she would wear as long as she remained a Vestal.

Of the six Vestal Virgins, two are small girls. It takes ten years to learn all the things they have to know, and another twenty before they can leave. They can be married then, if they like, though very few of them are.

Their main duty is to guard the sacred flame, which burns for ever on an altar in the exact place where the founders of Rome lit it originally. Though Antonia speaks so confidently about it, it's not always easy to keep that flame going, because there is a hole in the roof exactly above it, and sometimes rain falls so heavily that it is in real danger of being put out. The temple of the flame is round, to commemorate the round hut that stood there originally. One Vestal must stay on guard there always, day and night. Once a year, on the first of March, the flame is rekindled by rubbing a soft piece of dry wood against a hard piece cut from a fruit tree. When it blazes up, everyone knows that the City and the Empire will prosper for another year.

As well as guarding the sacred flame, the Vestals have charge of the little wooden statue of Pallas Athene, which was brought to Rome by Aeneas from Troy when that city was burnt. As Rome is in constant danger of being burnt too, the responsibility of guarding the statue is rather frightening, but it is kept in a secret store-room with some other treasures which are said to be equally valuable, though no one knows exactly what they are. All that is known is that as long as they are kept safe, Rome will last.

This month of June is the most important for the Vestals,

because the Vestalia, the feast of the goddess of fire, occurs on the ninth day of the month. On that day they begin to clean out their house, taking a week for it, and from the ninth until the fifteenth of the month, when all the dirt is disposed of, Romans feel that their city is in a dangerous position in relation to the gods.

Cleaning the temple of Vesta is part of the Vestals' work too, and special mops are used for it. The decorations of laurel are changed only once a year, on the first of March, after the sacred flame has been rekindled.

The Vestals have some sacrificial rites but they don't have to kill the animals themselves. The Roman idea of a sacrifice is that the god who is being honoured actually comes to the feast and eats the things that are cooked and offered to him. If it is a meat sacrifice, it is burnt and some wine thrown on the fire at the same time, and then the meat is eaten by the people who are attending the ritual. During the sacrifice, the priest says a prayer to the god, praising him or thanking him or asking for his help. The entrails—the liver, kidneys and heart —are always cooked separately and tasted before the feast begins, while the priest wears his toga over his head and musicians play special music.

All kinds of animals are sacrificed. The one that most concerns the Vestals is the October Horse, a religious rite which includes a chariot race and is held in the Forum on the fifteenth of October every year. Immediately the race is over, the priest of Mars, the god of war, slaughters the near horse of the winning pair and cuts off its head. The blood is collected in two pots, and one is poured at once over the hearth of the Emperor's house. The second pot is given to the Vestals, to be kept and used by them in their sacrifices during the year.

Not so long ago, people were sacrificed, but fortunately that custom has stopped. Instead, fish, cattle, sows, cocks, dogs, all kinds of birds, lambs, sheep, horses and donkeys are all slaughtered in the hope of pleasing the various gods. A special animal is thought to be pleasing to a certain god—for instance, Luna, the goddess of the moon, likes to have a dog, the sea-god, Neptune, likes horses, Favonius, the god of the wind, likes donkeys and so on. Some people believe that the god enters into the animal and that they are communicating with him when they eat it, but usually they don't eat dogs, horses nor donkeys.

Most of the things that the Vestals use for their sacrifices date back to the early times when the Romans were vegetarians and led a simple life. To commemorate those early founders of the City, the Vestals have to fetch water in jars from the sacred spring of Egeria, at the far end of the Forum. Egeria is the goddess of mothers and their babies, and the first Romans were always extremely anxious to preserve the population of the City from illness. Great numbers of people died because the mosquitoes brought malaria, and the children died of mysterious diseases of all kinds, mainly caused by lack of hygiene. The water from the fountain of Egeria was specially clean. No one got ill after drinking it and this may be the reason why it was thought to be holy.

The Vestals carry the jars on their heads and pour it into a special marble tank. Salt, which has been baked in an earthenware pot in an oven, is sprinkled into the tank before the water is used in the ceremonies. Special cakes with the same salt in them, baked by the Vestals, are made from the very first ears of wheat at the harvest, and this wheat has to be pounded into flour in a mortar, though the Romans have flour mills which would do the work much faster.

Antonia says that as well as their house, it is this ceremonial part of the Vestals' life that attracts her, much more so than the fact that they have places reserved for them at the games and can drive through the City like the priests. To go in every night to that quiet house, and sometimes to sit alone with the sacred fire, would be worth all the things one would have to give up in the outside world.

Quintus has spent a little too long in the Forum and now he hurries back with the sandals to his father. Today is a working day, which means that the family will go to the baths in the afternoon, but tomorrow is a full holiday when no public business is allowed and the stall can open only for an hour.

Back at the market, Licinia has some soup ready, with bread and cheese. The bread comes from the bakery of Camillus, Lepidus' cousin. He was a slave once but now he has three slaves of his own to help him with the work. He has a tiny ground-floor room in Pepper Street, with an oven in each of the two far corners. The oven is simply a wall of bricks built across the corner, with a charcoal fire on its floor. The front is open and the whole room is fearfully hot, so that whenever Quintus goes there to fetch the bread, he's afraid that he'll end by being baked himself.

The bread is mixed and raised and kneaded in front of the ovens on the floor, and it rises quickly because of the heat. Then the loaves are put on a kind of long-handled shovel, which a slave holds over the hot coals until the bread is baked. This takes about twenty minutes.

Camillus learned the trade of bakery in his master's house. Neither he nor his slaves are able to straighten their backs now, they have spent so much time on the stoop holding the shovels. Altogether baking is a very unhealthy occupation, the bakers' faces are white and drawn and it is well known that they die young. But the City must have bread, so various Emperors have offered inducements to anyone who will set up a bakery—freedom from taxes and gifts of money. Last year the present Emperor made several orders of this kind, and Lepidus suggested to Quintus that he might do worse than go to work with his cousin, but Quintus didn't like the idea at all. Roman fathers don't force their children to do things they don't want, so Lepidus didn't press the matter.

The loaf of bread is round, divided in four, made of a

mixture of whatever corn is cheapest—wheat and barley and oats, and perhaps even bean flour as well. The rich have pure wheat flour which makes white bread but the poor are glad to have anything at all. They get their bread free, by presenting vouchers which are given out every month, and this makes them less likely to complain of the quality.

When they have finished eating, the whole family tidies up the stall and Valeria sprinkles water around to lay the dust. Then they all lie down on the floor and sleep for an hour. It is so hot now that it's impossible to stay awake, in spite of the hard floor and the mosquitoes and flies that torment them. But in an hour or so, the mosquitoes win. A particularly vicious bite wakes Lepidus up and he rouses the whole family and tells them it's time to go to the baths.

Out of respect for Senator Flavius, they always try to go to the baths that he favours. They know he likes this, and indeed if he were nasty, instead of being the generous man he is, he could injure Lepidus in various ways if he thought he was no longer paying him proper attention. Lepidus knows that Flavius will always take an interest in him, so he makes sure to be seen as often as he can.

At the baths, though there are no class distinctions, Lepidus and his family stay close together at first so that they will be seen by their friends. Soon Quintus and Antonia will go off to play ball with friends who live near them, in Pomegranate Street, but they will come back later to go into the various rooms with their parents. In this way, they will be sure to get scraped and rubbed down by each other, since they have no slaves to do it for them.

As the afternoon goes on, everyone begins to look more healthy and cheerful. The park around the baths is so beautiful and the warm air so good that Quintus can feel his whole body get a new energy. Still, he always enjoys the Circus more than these quieter, healthier days at the baths. Tomorrow is a big feast day, and it is said that there will be five hundred gladiators at the Colosseum—a fairly modest number because it's only a religious feast. No one will ever forget the games that celebrated the present Emperor Trajan's Triumph over Decabalus, king of the Dacians, when five thousand gladiators fought and were killed in the Great Circus. It was only four years ago, and Quintus well remembers the triumphal procession. Many people were disappointed because Decabalus was not there, chained to the chariot wheels of the Emperor. He had killed himself when he was about to be captured.

Quintus is hardly aware that the gladiators are real men at all—for him it is as if they were toy soldiers. This impression is strengthened by the ceremonies that are used, the opening procession of gorgeously dressed gladiators and, as each one is killed, the figure of Charon that comes out to inspect the body and make sure that the man is really dead. These things all make the whole affair unreal.

The Emperor believes that the idle population of his capital city must be kept amused, else they will start to plot against the government. He spends more money on shows and spectacles than anyone has ever done before, and the people love him for it.

The Colosseum is used for ordinary shows but for really big days there is the Circus Maximus, which has been enlarged by different rulers over the years—Caesar, Augustus, Claudius, Nero and now Trajan—so that there is room for two hundred and fifty thousand spectators, sitting in tiers on stone seats. Underneath, in three arcades faced with marble, there are stalls where anyone with money can buy a glass of wine or a cake or some fruit to keep him alive during the long day.

At the Colosseum there is not so much seating, though it is the biggest Amphitheatre in all Rome. Until a hundred and fifty years ago, the shows took place in the Forum, inside a stockade which was taken away after each day's show. Then a rich man, wanting to get popular with the citizens, built two wooden theatres, semi-circular in the Roman style, set on swivels so that they could be used as two separate theatres with their curves touching at the back, or turned around so that their two flat sides came face to face to form an oval. The turning took place while the people were in their seats and everyone whooped with delight and fear as the whole theatre swung around. A short time afterwards, Caesar used the same plan, and it was only in 79 B.C. that a stone Amphitheatre was begun. This is the Colosseum that still stands in Rome, ten minutes' walk from Trajan's market and from Serpent Street where Quintus lives.

The fights that take place in the Colosseum are between men and animals or between men and men, or sometimes between one kind of animal and another. They go on from dawn to dusk, with as much variety as possible, and occasionally with real circus turns of the kind we know in our own time. There are panthers drawing chariots, elephants kneeling in front of the Emperor and drawing words in the dust with their trunks, tigers coming to lick the hand of their trainer, lions holding a live hare in their mouths and then releasing it unhurt.

But the spectacles that the people of Rome really love are those whose very memory disgusts us now, so that we can never understand how such civilised people could bring themselves to watch them at all, let alone fill the Amphitheatre on a hundred days of the year.

Perhaps Quintus doesn't really watch the show closely; perhaps he spends his time rambling around the huge alley-ways of the theatre, chatting to his friends, only turning his head now and then when the crowd shouts with extra excitement, but this is not likely. Most of the people get wildly excited and cheer and yell at the sight of the savage spectacle before them, much as the audiences do at the bull-fight in Spain and South America nowadays. This will go on

168

until the Christian Emperor Constantine puts a stop to it all on October 1st, 326, when he will say that criminals must no longer be sent to the arena but to work in the mines. After that, it will no longer be possible to keep the great gladiator barracks full of men, to be handed over to the promoters of the shows for a day's amusement.

There are several big theatres in Rome for the performance of plays but they are not plays as we know them now. The theatres are so big that most of the audience has no hope of hearing what the actors are saying, not because the sound doesn't travel but because the people won't stay quiet enough for the words to be heard. Twenty thousand is just too many in a theatre—the modern Opera House in Rome, which we would consider a huge theatre, holds only two thousand.

To make it possible for the audience to follow the play at all, symbols have been worked out which can be recognised by everyone. The actors wear masks, smiling or sad according to whether the play is a comedy or a tragedy, brown for men and white for women. The costumes show whom the actors are supposed to represent: a long white gown for an old man, purple for a rich one, striped for a young man, red for a poor man, a short, flowing cloak for a soldier, a short tunic for a slave and so on.

The actors speak lines, but there is a second actor, dressed like the principal one, who mimes the parts at the front of the stage to an accompaniment on a wind instrument, rather like a modern oboe except that it has two reeds side by side. Little by little the miming actors have realised that they can clown a bit and amuse the people at the actors' expense, and draw the attention to themselves. Naturally the actors don't like this, and there have been some nasty fights between actors and mimes because of it.

Some of the actors are so grand that they feel they own their mime, that he is a sort of shadow of themselves and must obey their every move, and in a way this is true.

So the plays have become more like ballets than straight plays, and soon they will be like opera as we know it nowadays, because an orchestra and choir are being added. There will still be dialogue, written by long-dead playwrights and usually on historical subjects, but interspersed with songs to the accompaniment of the orchestra, rather as Gilbert and Sullivan did later with their operas. There are songs in the plays now, and the crowds know the words—at Caesar's funeral they sang a famous one that begins: "Have I saved them only that they may kill me?"

Sometimes it happens that the audience disapproves of the way an actor interprets the part and they make him go back and do it again. Once when an actor was playing Agamemnon, he drew himself up to his full height to give himself extra greatness, and a voice from the audience called out:

"You're making him tall, not great!"

Everyone began to yell at him to go back and do it again, and he did, but this time he acted the part of a man bowed down in deep thought, indicating that a great man's business is to think for all the people. The audience cheered and clapped for a long time then, showing that they had appreciated the point.

Sometimes the rôles of mime and actor are reversed. One great actor who found that his voice was giving out has taken to miming his parts, while another one sings or speaks the words to an accompaniment on the flute.

In some ways, the Roman mimes are like the traditional Chinese theatre, in that they have a series of movements that are recognised by the audience to represent different things: spreading the fingers in the shape of a lyre to suggest music, feeling an imaginary pulse to suggest a sick person, bending the knees and taking long, slow steps to suggest fear and so on.

Unfortunately the plays that are performed are often as

171

disgusting as the shows in the Amphitheatre, with real cruelties and coarseness of a kind that is never allowed even in the most permissive of modern stage shows. One reason for this may be that in former times the various Emperors actually enjoyed the worst things and even took part in them. Nero liked acting, and disgraced himself over and over again by taking parts that were scandalous. On the other hand, when the Emperor Domitian's wife fell in love with the actor Paris, he divorced her.

The present Emperor does not approve of the goings on in the theatre but he does nothing about it, because above all things he wants to keep the people occupied.

Gradually the Romans are finding historical, poetic plays too dull, with their upright, tragic characters. They prefer plays about their own daily lives, and there is a new playwright who writes very much to their taste—"The Mother-in-Law" and "The Aunt" are two of his plays, with plenty of jokes that everyone will understand and lots of wrestling and pie-throwing. These plays are written as fast as they are needed—one playwright wrote four in sixteen days. The actors are very skilful at improvising and adding references to things that are happening in the City and the Court, though they are careful not to insult the Emperor. That would be to risk their skins.

As there are no changes of scene, interest has to be provided in other ways. For instance, in a play about Agamemnon, six hundred mules were led across the stage to represent his plunder. It must have looked rather like a present-day summer performance of Verdi's "Aïda", in the Baths of Caracalla at Rome, where hundreds of actors dressed as Roman soldiers crowd the stage and the climax comes when a *biga*—a two-horse chariot—is driven at speed up the centre, to the sound of trumpets and the full orchestra and chorus.

Apart from plays and circuses, on feast days the people love a day's outing. On the Lupercalia, the 15th of February, the day begins with the sacrifice of goats and dogs in honour of the god Faunus, at a cave called the Lupercal below the Palatine Hill, where perhaps Romulus and Remus were fed by the she-wolf. Afterwards, boys run around the City striking everyone they meet, especially women, with strips of the goat-skins, and the day ends with crowds walking about the streets eating, drinking wine and singing or dancing.

On July 23rd there is the feast of Neptune, when people go to the seashore and spend the day there, or to the river-bank if they can't get as far as the sea. They build shelters of the boughs of trees, as modern Romans do, and sing the songs they have heard at the theatre or popular songs, and the women dance, letting down their long hair. Later they eat and drink, and come home in the evening exhausted.

The Saturnalia is a seven-day celebration, beginning on December 17th and going on to the 24th. While it lasts, the slaves take over the houses and the masters serve them with their meals, and there are special games that the children play, one of them being "King of the Castle". But nothing is really organised for these days: it's a time when people do whatever they like. No one knows who the god Saturnus is, but everyone agrees that his feast is the most cheerful one in the whole year.

The ceremonies for the feast of Jupiter on the 13th of September are much more solemn. Jupiter has the most important temple in Rome, on the Capitol looking down on the Forum. The celebrations start from there, with a procession. In front there are small boys marching, then older ones on horses, then the chariots that are going to take part in the races, with the charioteers dressed in their colours, then dancers and flute-players, and last of all the image of the god himself, carried on a specially made platform.

The whole town comes out to watch, and follows the band down to the Circus Maximus for the races. There is nothing to pay, so everyone can go. Usually the judge in charge of the day's entertainment has to dig into his own pocket to pay for some of the fun, but most of it comes out of the public purse. Especially since the last campaign in Dacia, Rome is very rich, but if the money were to run out, then the people in the provinces would be taxed more heavily, because at all costs the Romans must be entertained.

Apart from sending money, the Roman provinces must supply the animals for the games, panthers and lions and tigers and elephants. One provincial Governor gets so many demands for panthers that he's afraid the species will die out altogether. All the governors point out that catching these animals takes time—they don't come when they're called, but must be hunted for days on end, slowly and cautiously, to catch them alive.

The ordinary Roman citizen doesn't care where the fun comes from so long as there's plenty of it.

Though so many of the games and races and celebrations are held in the name of religion, it is doubtful if the people have any real belief in the gods. Everywhere the temples are falling to pieces from neglect, except in the neighbourhood of the Forum where they must be kept up for show. The soldiers who have come back from the wars have heard of other, more interesting gods—there have been many converts to the worship of Mithras, the Persian sun-god, and also to the Egyptian religion of Isis. She is the goddess of the Nile and has the virtues of all the gods. Her husband is Osiris, who was once a Pharaoh. When he died, he was brought back to life and now reigns in the underworld. Through him, men and animals can be brought to everlasting life.

Though Christianity is not allowed in Rome, the cult of Isis and Osiris is tolerated. There are temples to them in many cities, with special platforms for performing the ceremonies and tanks for the Nile water that forms a part of them, as well as cells for the priests to live in. It is a peaceful religion and doesn't interfere with the people's allegiance to the Emperor as Christianity could do.

For the ordinary man, these are far better religions than the traditional Roman one, with its fierce gods who have to be placated with sacrifices all the time and who do nothing much in return. It will be two hundred years before Christianity takes over, with its central idea of a god of love, concerned for the happiness and welfare of even the weakest people. The Romans will take to the new ideas with enthusiasm, because at heart they are a cheerful, well-meaning people with a great capacity for enjoying life.

Quintus respects the old gods and he is taking no chances with them. Now and then, he goes to consult the oracle at the shrine of Fortune on the Quirinal Hill at the top of Serpent Street. The oracle is not a human person, like the old woman at Puteoli near Neapolis, and it costs nothing to go in and find out what is in store for one. There is a box before the image of the goddess, with little pieces of oakwood in it, and words inscribed on each. Quintus slips in quietly and gets the attendant boy to pick one out. Every time, the words are the same: "Jupiter fills his store." Quintus takes this to mean that he is going to succeed in business as Marcus has done, though it could equally well mean that he is going to die young, or that he is going to be a priest in a temple, or even a general in the army.

On this lovely June evening, as they all stroll home from the baths together, he is not too worried about the future. Tomorrow can take care of itself, so long as today has sunshine and good soup and bread, and some fun and games at the end of it. The moon is rising, the goddess Luna, bringing with her ghosts and evil spirits of all kinds, though she brings good things to women and babies, and success in war and business to some. She gives the only light in Rome by night, and as she is full tonight, the people can sleep easy in their beds. On dark nights, thieves prowl the City like cats, and as the family hurry upstairs to their apartment, the hall-way is already dark enough to be terrifying. On the other hand, it would be a tough thief indeed who could stand there hiding, with that smell.

Inside their room it's a little better. They stand for a moment before the shrine of the Lares, and Lepidus says a short prayer of thanks for having got through the day alive. Then they pull out the mattresses and lie down in their clothes, to sleep until another dawn.